For Norma

THE MAN UPSTAIRS

Mark L. Fowler

With Best Wishes

Mark

A CIP catalogue record for this title is available from the British Library.

For Joe and Fiona

ONE: THE MAYOR, THE MAN UPSTAIRS AND THE GIRL IN THE BLUE PYJAMAS

The phone rang for the second time that night. I hadn't liked the first call and I had the feeling that I wasn't going to like this one any better. There was trouble coming to Chapeltown. Big trouble. Trouble with a capital T.

Don't get me wrong - trouble was coming to the right place. Trouble was my business. Yet there was something in the air that I hadn't felt before, the vibrations thundering down the track like a ghost train from hell. The cut-out sun had gone down on a universe out of kilter and TMU, The Man Upstairs, the god pulling all the strings had inexplicably let the stars slip out of alignment. It should never have been left to his creations to shuffle the firmament back into some kind of order.

I took the call.

The voice on the other end of the line belonged to a woman who had no place in my world. A woman named Marge. She wore blue pyjamas and she was further proof that TMU was losing the plot.

I told the woman it was late and that it would have to wait. She was saying that it couldn't wait. She was always saying that it couldn't wait.

While her voice rolled on I looked out of my window to see a fat old man, his face at least, smiling crookedly down at me through so many thousand miles of empty black space. Mad old moon, cut and pasted onto the Chapeltown sky.

The woman was becoming hysterical. I told her that I was on my way when I should have told her to jump out of the window.

Driving across town I thought about the other call. The earlier one. It was from a woman who spoke in whispers. She didn't wish to disclose her name, though she knew mine the same as she knew my number. She had a tale to tell. A tale about a care worker by the name of Nancy Tate.

Nancy had been working for the Chapeltown Angels. One evening after she'd finished her shift she paid a visit to the Town Hall. Later that same evening, shortly after leaving the Town Hall a hit and run driver ended her short life.

Our infamous police department never caught the driver and concluded that her death was best filed under 'Tragic Accidents'. The anonymous woman on the phone had come to a very different conclusion. She thought that Nancy Tate's death was murder.

I asked the whispering woman if she had anyone in mind for the killing.

She did, as it happened. Thomas Jackson.

Not a man to get his hands dirty, apparently, this Thomas Jackson; but still, according to the whispering woman, he was the one who arranged it.

The name didn't ring any bells and so I asked who this Thomas Jackson was.

"Are you kidding?"

I wasn't and I said so.

"Well, I don't know where you've been hiding lately, but Thomas Jackson is the elected Mayor of Chapeltown," she told me.

"Chapeltown has an elected mayor?"

The laugh that followed suggested that her previous whispering was caused neither by illness nor disability, but rather the wish to remain anonymous. And discretion's fine. I've been known to use it myself on occasions.

I said, "It sounds like your throat's getting better. They say laughter is the best medicine. So how long has Chapeltown had an elected mayor?"

This time she didn't laugh.

"Okay," I said, "so why would this Mayor of Chapeltown – this Thomas Jackson - arrange to have a care worker killed?"

It was back to whispers.

She told me, this whispering enigma, how Jackson had hit the ground running, wasting no time extending his civic duties to the town's young ladies.

One too many of them.

Nancy Tate, an enterprising girl, thought he ought to pay for his fun and promptly wound up dead. The police did what the police generally do in Chapeltown, which involves a lot of paperwork but very little police work, concluding that accidents happen and leaving Jackson to carry on playing at being mayor. Leaving those who knew Nancy Tate to say their goodbyes and resign themselves to the vagaries of an uncertain world.

"So Nancy was blackmailing him?"

"I didn't say that."

"Not in so many words. Listen, I need to speak to you in person –"

"No!"

The whisper had slipped again. The voice came out raw.

"What are you afraid of?" I asked. "You think you might be next?"

"I can't tell you anything more than I've told you already."

"Are you sure about that?"

She hesitated. "You should visit Alice Coor."

"Who's Alice Coor?"

"She works for the Chapeltown Angels."

The phone clicked and the whisperer was gone, back into the savage night.

I crossed the haunted landscape and headed into the centre, the Town Hall grinning out of the night like a clown at a dark carnival. I wondered if the mayor was working late. If I hadn't been engaged on more 'pressing matters' I might have paid him a visit. Might have dropped in to ask why he hadn't seen fit to let Chapeltown's most famous dweller, Frank Miller, the *Yours Truly* of this sorry tale, know about his recent appointment.

I thought over what the whispering woman had said and none of it rang true. *Chapeltown taking it upon itself to appoint a mayor, then this same guy immediately setting about the young women with a vengeance and silencing the first one to squeal.*

No, I didn't like it. Didn't buy it for a second. It was like something straight out of a cheap crime mystery thriller. Bargain basement junk that The Man Upstairs always professed to have no time for.

As for the whisperer getting nothing from the police, well, that *did* ring true. As a general rule nobody ever got anything out of them. That's when the good people of Chapeltown find themselves turning to Frank Miller himself, and knowing that they've done the right thing as soon as they catch sight of him riding into town in his Datsun Cherry...

I'd been driving that tired old jalopy since The Man Upstairs first set pen to paper and came up with the name Frank Miller. He'd tried me out in Vegas, Venice, Rome, London, even Sydney, Australia. But none of those towns worked. So he made up a place for me and

8

called it Chapeltown. And before you could say "Old-School PI living on broads and booze", the first Frank Miller mystery was out on sale.

Twenty books down the line and I'm still on sale, though I'm the only character in this town of the damned that seems to know the set up.

My old Datsun wheezed up Hill Street and spluttered out at the Honeywall Flats. I looked up to see the light in the third floor window.

Over the course of twenty books The Man Upstairs had given me nothing but one-night stands and I was not complaining. That was the Frank Miller style and not I, my readers, not even the ladies concerned had an issue with it. Yet here I was, three months into late night calls at the Honeywall Flats, answering the whistle like a faithful mutt.

I went through the broken door and up the stone steps.

Reaching the green door with the number 33 written on in black marker, I used the knuckles of my legendary right hand to tap out my trademark rhythm. It was the theme from an old western that had once formed the basis of my education.

Marge answered the door as though I was from the TV detection agency, her alabaster face peeping out at me with an expression poised between pleading and innocence. I said, "It's Frank. I was under the impression that you were expecting me."

I could see she'd been crying. She let me in and I went through to the living room and sat down on the big yellow sofa. She came in behind me and wouldn't you know it, she was wearing those blue pyjamas again. The television was on but the sound was muted. Some film was showing but I didn't recognise it. A lot of people seemed to be getting in and out of cars and there were a lot of serious faces and quite a few guns pointing here and there. I imagined that with the sound on it would have been a noisy affair.

"Practicing your lip reading?" I said, pointing at the silent screen.

"It's on for the *company*, Frank."

Marge didn't use words idly.

"Three months," she said, sitting two cushions away from me.

"Who would have thought it," I said. "Were you expecting flowers?"

"Why do you have to be like that all the time?"

"I wasn't being funny, Marge. Look, what's this about?"

She looked ready to slap my face. It wouldn't have been the first time. Then her expression softened, her voice bubbling with tears. "We're getting along okay, aren't we, Frank?"

Before I could say anything she was crying - big sobs, too. I covered the distance of two cushions and my arm did the right thing, wrapping itself around her shoulders. She looked up at me with those full eyes dripping and I thought about the girl in the fist of King Kong.

I'd watched that film with Marge a dozen times, though I could never see the point of it. Maybe she was trying to tell me something about Beauty and the Beast, but if that was the case then I'm afraid that I was too dumb to catch it.

Out it came. How she thought we had something special. How she wanted more than me just calling around when I had the "inclination".

'Summoned' would have been a better description.

I kept the thought to myself. I was waiting for the C word. She used every synonym for that treacherous word but left 'commitment' hanging like a noose.

The way she went about assassinating my character made we wonder if this wasn't the end. If she wasn't about to send me back out into the night and let me get on with living the only life I knew how to live.

The wrong kind.

The Frank Miller kind.

"…You're nothing but a walking cliché, Frank."

"I'm who I am, Marge. Nothing more and nothing less. It's how I was made."

"But you can change, Frank."

Now I got it and it was the oldest story in the book. A woman falls in love with a man and straight away sets about trying to change him. But sometimes it just can't be done.

"To change me would be to kill me."

"Not that old line, Frank."

"I'm serious."

"What are you talking about?"

"I'm talking about The Man Upstairs."

"Upstairs? Where upstairs? Believing in God now, are we? So you can blame *Him* for how you turned out!"

She was on the button. God/ The Man Upstairs - they amounted to the same thing in Chapeltown. TMU had made her as surely as he'd made everybody else in this town, but I didn't plan on being the one to break the news. It wasn't down to me to tell her just what her life amounted to – and certainly not while she was wearing those blue pyjamas. Those things should have come with a licence. Their effect on me was nothing short of lethal. And now the water in her big brown eyes had puffed those peepers up so full that I wanted to dive down into them.

So that's what I did: went brown-eyes diving. And in no time her heart was hammering so loud I couldn't hear my own above the din. The bedroom was ten feet away and it didn't take us long to get there.

And then time and space yielded to the Chapeltown night.

She was back in her blue pyjamas and I was wrapped up in the matching cotton robe she had bought to celebrate our first month together. The muted television screen was still throwing shadows around the flat, and dim echoes of the unspoken C word and its spoken synonyms still reverberated around the room as we made small talk about the joys and terrors of the world as we knew it. I didn't know whether to envy or pity her. All she knew was...*this.* For her there was no TMU.

I caught myself looking at her, wondering what I was doing spending a cozy evening in with a girl who wore an old lady's bedclothes. Frank Miller had never been one for the homely 'girl-next-door' type. Frank went for the vixens in fishnets; the devils in blue dresses and red garters, thorns without even the promise of a rose.

So what was TMU trying to pull? His readers wanted the old Frank, the despicable me out sniffing for the painted creatures of the night, not some steady boyfriend conspiring with romantic evenings spent in the company of a plain Jane wearing grandma's linens.

All the same she looked good in them.

Too good.

What was The Man Upstairs playing at?

At some stage those wretched blue Frank-teasers were off again and all time went back to the moon.

We woke up early. Marge had to go to work. She told me I could stay in bed and let myself out later. I had an afternoon appointment with Alice Coor, as recommended by the whispering woman. My morning was free though. I pulled Marge to me and told her to ring in.

"I have to work for a living, Frank. Unless you're planning on taking me away from all this. Make an honest woman of me, Frank. Take me out of Chapeltown and show me the world."

But Chapeltown *was* the world. For the likes of Marge and me there was nothing else.

I watched her tail disappear through the bedroom door and when I heard the shower kick in, pouring water on all of my dreams, I was about ready to put a fist through the window to restore a sense of equilibrium.

All done up for the hospital she came back into the bedroom and gave me the sweetest, most innocent peck on the cheek. Then she looked down and saw what was lurking beneath the sheets.

"Never gives you any rest, does it?" she said.

Wasn't *that* the truth!

"I've got to go, Frank. I'll call you later."

"Wait a minute," I said. "Since when did Chapeltown elect itself a mayor?"

"Since everybody voted for him."

"I didn't vote."

"That's up to you."

"But you voted?"

"Bye, Frank."

13

The door closed behind her, leaving the flat as emptied of life as the story book pages The Man Upstairs calls the universe. A dark, cold feeling swept through me. One I hadn't encountered before. I almost went after her. The urge to share the burden of this secret life lived in public was suddenly overwhelming.

I knew little about Marge. TMU had chosen to provide me with mere scraps. I'd never seen her outside of the flat. She told me that she went off every day to be a nurse at the Chapeltown General. But what else did I know?

I knew nothing.

I thought about her as I lay on that bed – though I wasn't thinking the way I usually did. I was thinking that it was a poor excuse for a life TMU had given her. She was hardly more than a sketch; a part-creation. For the reader she existed here, in this one place, and she always would and that was the extent of it.

And yet she had been given the role of trying to change the unchangeable Frank Miller. That was some undertaking for a minor player. What was he playing at? Had he forgotten the rules or was he just choosing to disregard them?

With one stroke of his pen TMU could wipe Marge out of existence. He could do the same for me, for that matter, though why would he? Where would that leave him? I was his bread and butter – the creation that had made him famous. I was the one he had tasked with telling his weird stories. If he killed me off there was nothing left.

I thought again about Marge, leaving the page; trading in her blue pyjamas for a hospital day-job uniform. To live or not live out an off-page life that was neither here nor there.

Maybe it was time that Marge knew the truth about Frank Miller and about the world that TMU had created. Maybe it was time for me to share the pitiful reality of existence with one other person in Chapeltown.

Yet I couldn't do it. Didn't think she could stand the knowledge.

For the first time I thought about what it would be like to live as somebody else. Empathy, I think they call it, though there's precious little of it in this shrunken world of mine. Still, I tried it and for a few moments I was Marge, sitting there in that big empty bed, believing in a bigger reality; of a place beyond these tormented streets and broken lives – and it made me want to cry.

I lay back and thought about what she wanted. What she was asking of me.

No, it couldn't be done.

It was impossible.

To change Frank Miller?

The public would never allow it.

It would kill the series.

And if the series was dead then so was Frank.

And Marge...

TWO: ALICE

I left the Honeywall Flats and walked out into the uneasy sunshine. I'd folded up Marge's blue pyjamas and placed them on her pillow, a big part of me wanting to wait for her shift at the Chapeltown General to finish.

Waiting for her to come back from being somebody else's nursemaid so that I could serve up something that I'd been cooking inside me all day.

In twenty Frank Miller mysteries TMU hadn't put a foot wrong, and neither had I. Yet here I was, aching to be a house-pet for a girl I wouldn't have looked twice at in any of my previous adventures.

But if the scene with Marge was all wrong, it was nothing compared to this Jackson case that TMU had cooked up. Why did Chapeltown suddenly want to elect a mayor? And why didn't I know anything about it?

Pointing my faithful Datsun Cherry back down Hill Street, I thought over my last few cases. They had been the business: murder, blackmail, twists, double twists, double cross and triple bluff; mystery, suspense and endless one-night stands with Chapeltown's dirtiest. No complaints and plenty to cherish.

I let my thoughts roam back to the early days, even before I knew about TMU. In those days the jobs were nothing but fun, if becoming a touch predictable, perhaps. Straightforward tales designed to tax the reader about as much as they taxed the writer. TMU could have written them standing on his head, and for all I know he probably had done. Maybe he'd written them two at a time with a pen in each hand.

I don't know about that. But sales had certainly been slowing down and the critics had been having regular field days at TMU's expense.

Then one day a job came up that didn't ring true. Just like this present case didn't ring true. A job that was different from all the others and one that for a long while I couldn't get any angle on at all. It turned out to be the best seller of the series: the now legendary case of *The Black Widow*.

It was working on *The Black Widow* that got me curious about what I was doing in Chapeltown. About who was behind it all, pulling the strings, so to speak. That's when I found out about TMU, and once I knew about him, the rest fell into place: Who I was and what my role in this substitute for a real life amounted to. Then the work really took off and the sales with it. All the best days were still ahead of me, as it turned out, and it's been that way ever since.

Until now.

The road out to the Estates took me back past the Town Hall. The dark carnival grin hadn't sobered up, despite the glare of morning, and even in daylight it was enough to give you the creeps. I wasn't sad to see it reducing to nothing in my rear view mirror.

A couple of miles out on the East Chapel road brought me to the Central Chapel Estate. It was a place scorpions refused to inhabit and it was home to Alice Coor.

I tapped out a hardboiled rhythm on a faecal-brown door and a few moments later a frowning figure from the rough end of Hades appeared.

I'd looked up the Chapeltown Angels following the anonymous call from the Whisperer, and asked to speak to Alice Coor. Her phone manner tended to move

17

back and forth between sickly sweet and downright abrasive, and the mention of the death of her colleague, Nancy Tate, seemed to bring out the worst in her.

She ushered me inside her little palace.

Alice Coor turned out to be a slim and not entirely unattractive woman, though her features had the toughened look of metal that had been plunged into the trough too quickly. I wondered if the shrunken top and belt-style skirt was the normal daytime attire of the semi-widowed housewife around those parts. It wouldn't have surprised me either way.

She made some coffee that I didn't like the look of and sat the two of us down in opposing seats. Then she told me enough about herself to make me thankful that I still had Marge to go back to.

Alice Coor, it seemed, had been through a number of husbands, and it didn't sound to me like any of them would be looking back fondly on the memories. The current Mr. Coor was looking at me from the inside of a car-boot picture frame that took pride of place on a TV set big enough to serve the Chapeltown picture house. His image made me think of heavyweight boxers and bandages. They clearly belonged together, the handsome couple, and my only wish for their future was that it had little to do with mine.

Coor felt the need to assure me that her man was a long-distance driver and that he could be away for long stretches. It was at that point that I contrived to bring the conversation around to Nancy.

"Nancy Tate was a whore," said Alice Coor, chewing – or at least pretending to chew – a mouthful of gum while slurping at the hot, brown stew in the mug she was holding in her fist. "Just a dirty fucking whore."

"I believe she was a Chapeltown Angel. That she worked for the same agency that you work for – is that correct?"

Alice Coor's face darkened. "What are you trying to say?"

"I'm trying to establish the facts."

"She was a care worker, same as me. Work all hours and the pay's shit. But you don't do it for the pay. You do it because you care. You do it for *love*. At least I do. Can't talk for scum like Tate."

Appearances can be deceptive and you can't always judge a book by the cover - and I speak with some authority on the matter, living life between the covers that TMU chooses to adorn his masterpieces. That said, Alice Coor didn't strike me as somebody who would do *anything* for love.

"Tate might have worked for the same agency as me, but that's all we had in common. Like I say, she was a whore, pure and simple."

Her eyes never left mine, like she was daring me to contradict her.

I said, "My understanding is that Nancy Tate was the victim of a hit-and-run. I believe she was working on the evening in question –"

"Correct. An accident. But I'm losing no sleep over it. I think you get what you deserve in this world. Don't you agree?"

"Sometimes," I said. "Then again, sometimes not. Do you think Nancy Tate was blackmailing Thomas Jackson?"

"What would she have to blackmail him with?"

"You don't believe that our new mayor has any skeletons in his cupboards, then?"

"I'll tell you what I believe, shall I?"

"If it's no trouble. That would be helpful."

19

"I believe that Thomas Jackson is the best thing that ever happened to Chapeltown."

I winced a little at that, I have to admit. Didn't Alice Coor realise that I'd spent twenty books trying to put Chapeltown straight? In this town full of losers there was only one hero and she was looking straight at him.

"You want the truth – I'll tell you the truth. Nancy Tate was a small time hooker with big ideas to blackmail her way to fame and riches."

"So she *was* blackmailing Jackson?"

Coor was on her feet, her metal face welding into the shape of a crowbar. There was pain behind those eyes, and the willingness to inflict it. "Are you calling me a liar?"

The seconds ticked loudly and I waited on every last one of them. After a while she seemed to recognise the futility of her outburst. She sat down and smiled. It wasn't the most re-assuring of smiles. It was the kind of smile people get in the moments before they receive the bullet to the back of the head. "Sorry," she said. "I get worked up sometimes. Can't control my temper, it's a weakness of mine. Where were we?"

"Still trying to establish the facts," I said.

"The facts are that bitch thought she could use Thomas Jackson."

"But you don't believe she had anything on him?"

"She couldn't have. The man's a saint."

I looked for traces of irony but didn't find any.

"So you don't think blackmailing Jackson cost Nancy Tate her life?"

"How many times do I have to say it? Thomas Jackson's what this town needs. And this town's better off without the likes of Nancy Tate. Her death was an accident, but you won't find me or any of the other girls fretting. Go and ask them – don't take my word for it."

"I might just do that," I said. "Do you have any names and addresses to start me off?"

Her eyes were burning with what TMU sometimes described as 'malignant intent'. I could see why the scorpions refused to live on this estate, not daring to share the same air as the likes of Alice Coor.

"Want another drink, Mr. Detective?"

"I'm okay, thanks. I don't need to keep you – if you could maybe just write down -"

"Mind if I make myself one?"

There was a twinkle in her eye that hadn't been there before. One that looked well practiced. She took my cup away and I wasn't the least bit sad to see it leave. I watched her go into the kitchen. That skirt certainly was short and didn't she know it.

I was starting to relax a little. Starting to feel the old twitches re-asserting themselves. This was shaping up into good old Frank Miller territory after all. Nice and sleazy. Alice Coor was starting to look less like a threat and more like a challenge. Maybe The Man Upstairs was approaching it all from a different angle. Wrong footing the reader. Getting ready to spring one of those famous Frank Miller moments.

So why was I sitting there, thinking about Marge and the promise of those wretched blue pyjamas? And what was it with those damned things? I didn't get why I was so taken with them. It was all part of Marge's homeliness, making her stand apart from the heartless witches that I usually got mixed up with.

The likes of Alice Coor for instance.

Marge wasn't that kind and never could be. Marge was the kind you settle down with, not take what you can get from. And what's the good of that for a guy like me? In every other book in the series I would have been on the likes of Alice Coor like a rash and to hell with the consequences.

Coor returned with another mug of sludge.

She stood in the doorway. "So why are you here, anyway? The police already looked into that slag's death and they decided it was an accident. Somebody told you different?"

"That would be telling."

"So tell me."

"There's nothing to tell, at least not yet."

"So why are you here?"

"To do the asking."

"So ask away."

I stood up. "I have a medical condition."

"Anything serious?" she asked, though with no hint of any real concern.

"Serious enough. You see, if I start to go around in circles I get nauseous, so you must excuse me."

I moved towards the door.

"You don't want names, then, *Frank*?"

Those eyes. Those lips. That look. *Vicious.*

I was weakening.

Just not quite enough.

I stayed not a minute longer than it took to get the name and address of another girl from the agency. A fellow Chapeltown Angel by the name of Michelle Spar. Alice Coor told me that if I wanted to know more about Nancy Tate, Michelle was the one to see.

As I was leaving Coor asked if I would need to visit her again. I said that I might and left it at that. Then she reminded me that her husband was away and that she was available for at least the rest of the week.

That twinkle was in her eye again. Except that 'twinkle' doesn't come close to capturing what was hiding on the other side of that look. A lot of work had gone into that look and over many years, I didn't doubt it. Yet despite the professionalism at work she still couldn't conceal the hidden crowbar.

"If Nancy Tate's death was just an accident, then I won't have any reason to come back and see you," I said.

"Oh, but you will, Frank."

"Why's that?"

"You're a sucker for my kind of company every bit as much as I'm a sucker for a man in a raincoat."

"Is that a fact?"

"That's a fact, Frank."

We left it at that.

I made arrangements to meet Michelle Spar that evening. It should have been grist to the mill.

So why could I only think about getting the job done and out the way and heading back to see Marge? Marge was there any time. Marge was the TV dinner when the fire in the kitchen closed the restaurant for the night.

What game was Dr. Frankenstein playing?

THREE: MICHELLE

I parked the trusty Cherry outside a condemned block on the East Chapel Road at the stroke of seven. Michelle Spar lived on the ground floor of a block of flats in need of a wrecking ball, yet somehow she had managed to make hers stand out from its neighbours, and not in a good way. At least the obscene graffiti on the door lessened the shock of actually stepping foot over the threshold.

Amidst the general squalor that greeted me inside the flat stood Michelle Spar, done up like the dinner only a ravenous dog could dream about.

Her perfume was like a punch on the nose, and when she lit up the first cigarette the combination raised up an image of what I'd feared was a long gone Frank Miller.

The old Frank Miller.

The hero of a series of outrageous adventures, living out an eternal youth in a timeless golden age. Six foot of lean muscle and slicked back hair that looked just about right in a PI's raincoat. A cynical smile that no amount of whisky and bad living could dismantle. A character that hordes of corrupt females could never compromise – need I go on?

They were simple enough pleasures taken in what now, in retrospect, seemed like innocent times. Times stretching back before the days of the *Black Widow*; before the glory days darkened at the hand of TMU, creating a fallen version of a once-perfect world where once-upon-a-time everything could be taken for granted, and where nothing ever could again.

Spar seemed to have difficulty maintaining eye contact, but she did show off an impressive drinks cabinet. It was clearly her pride and joy.

I agreed to sample some of the whisky in the unmarked bottle, to put her at ease.

While she poured out a stiff one I cast a detective's eye around my immediate environment. There wasn't much to report; there wasn't much of anything. The flat had as much of a condemned feel to it on the inside as it did on the outside, making it a home from home as far as I was concerned. Time was when TMU had given me a flat and an office. But lately he was thinning things down, like there were cutbacks in the air or something. I was living in a hole that comprised a bed, a chair and a phone. Was that any way to treat a hero?

I digress.

She handed me a glass and the taste took me straight back. I was Frank Miller again. I waited for the warmth to spread to my guts and then I got down to business.

"I believe that you know Thomas Jackson?"

She was lacing into a large vodka that I didn't imagine to be her first of the evening.

"Are you trying to be funny, Mr -"

"The name's Frank. And no, I gave up trying to be funny when the world lost its sense of humour. Like I said on the phone, I'm here to investigate the death of Nancy Tate. Your colleague, Alice Coor, seems to think Nancy's death was an accident and nothing to do with the mayor."

"You don't waste time, do you?"

"Not as a rule."

"Who says it was anything to do with Thomas Jackson?"

It was a reasonable question. I could have said that a woman whispering down my phone line told me, but I didn't feel the need. Instead I said, "Of course there is another line of speculation – that Thomas Jackson's practically a saint."

"He's not done anything wrong that I know of."

"That's unusual," I said. "For a man in high office, I mean."

I'd done enough talking. It was time to open up a space and let her fill it with what she knew.

For the next five minutes, and without leaving her drinks trolley once, she warbled around a retelling of what I'd already heard from Coor. About Nancy Tate being a slag and a chancer and generally no loss to the people of Chapeltown.

When she saw how unimpressed I was she tried some extracts from her autobiography, mostly taken from the section on divorce, terminated pregnancies and childhood bereavement. It wasn't the most uplifting tale I'd ever heard.

The drinks were going down fast over by the trolley and I wondered whether it might be better to make another appointment. She was taking the liquor well, though, and her story was beginning to shape up, despite all the refreshments.

"I got the job at the agency and I was keeping my head above water, just about. I met him at one of his fund raising afternoons. He gave this speech and I thought he was like the king or God or something. Everybody loved him. Afterwards there was a buffet, and he was doing the rounds, talking to staff, giving it all the chat. I could tell straight off that he was one for the ladies. You know what I mean?"

I nodded. As portraits go, it wasn't exactly unique around Chapeltown.

"Anyway, he seemed to zoom straight in on the pretty ones, and I could tell he was working out more than how well they could change an incontinence pad."

26

She topped up the vodka and I allowed myself another shot of ruin to celebrate the progress we were making.

"I knew I was one of the girls he'd got his eye on. He didn't say much, but he handed me his card. He said that the town needed more people like me and that he meant to use the town's natural resources to turn things around. He didn't know me, didn't hear me say a word. I was pretty certain that ringing that number was going to do nothing for the general health of this town."

"And did it?"

"I tell you, he was a perfect gentleman. He spent time with me but he wasn't after anything, if you know what I mean."

"What made you ring the number?"

"Curiosity, I suppose. He said he believed that people were Chapeltown's greatest resource, and that by investing in them we would all reap the rewards. He was always coming out with stuff like that."

"And you believed him?"

"Of course I didn't. But like I said, I was curious. I mean, I think it was a brave thing to do, inviting someone like me to meet him in private."

"Brave?"

"Well, I mean, after all, a man in his position inviting a young woman to meet him privately – that's the kind of thing that can get a mayor a bad name."

It certainly was. I looked at Michelle, trying to weigh up if she was for real. The jury was out. I asked her, "What do you suppose anybody might gain by falsely accusing the mayor of murder?"

She didn't answer, instead taking an exaggerated wiggle over towards the great unwashed window that was letting a few dirty trickles of late sunshine into her world. I waited until she'd turned back around and then I asked her again.

"You don't think it unreasonable that someone like Nancy Tate could have been blackmailing Thomas Jackson? She sounds like the type, from what I'm hearing. That would give our lovely new mayor a motive for murder, wouldn't it?"

"You've got it all wrong."

"Which part have I got wrong? That Nancy was the type to blackmail a newly elected dignitary, or that the aforementioned Thomas Jackson was the type to respond by killing her – or at least arranging to have her killed?"

"Are you taking the piss?"

"I would never do that."

"What do you want?"

I placed the drink down on the small table next to me. "I want you to answer me, truthfully. Do you think Nancy's death was an accident or do you think it was murder?"

"I think that Nancy Tate can rot in hell."

"So I'm getting the idea that you two were not exactly pals. What was it, Michelle? Why did you hate her so much?"

"She was trouble."

"What kind of trouble?"

"She tried to take my man."

"I see."

"No you don't. She tried to take my man, telling him stuff that wasn't true. She made up things about me. She didn't want him, not really, she just didn't want me to have him. She was like that. She couldn't bear to see anybody else happy."

"Do you think others felt the same way about her?"

"I can't speak for anybody else."

"She sounds to me like the kind of person who could make life very difficult for a man in a position of power and authority."

"I know what you're trying to say."

"Jackson had Nancy Tate killed, didn't he?"

Michelle was staring at me hard and gripping the glass in her hand like she was bent on breaking it. Then her expression softened. "You know something?" she said. "I'm glad you came here tonight, Frank."

"Really? Why's that?"

"I wasn't sure I'd be able to talk to you, but you can open a woman up just like shelling peas."

It was an oddly phrased compliment, though I'd taken worse.

"I'm just doing my job," I said, "Oh, and getting nicely confused."

"I haven't told anybody else about how that bitch tried to take my man, but I can talk to you, Frank. You make me want to unload."

I finished off the whisky in my glass. It was helping - helping make sense of Michelle Spar at least. I was beginning to feel like that ravenous dog. Feeling like the real Frank Miller again.

"Another drink, Frank?"

I looked at my watch, though only for the sake of appearances. The thing about detective work is that you never know how long a job's likely to take. Frank Miller, whilst indisputably courteous and chivalrous to a fault, is not and never has been above recognising that the female of the species can perpetrate the most heinous crimes with only the merest prompting from the three-headed monster of means, motive and opportunity.

With this in mind I came to a decision.

A Frank Miller decision.

"Okay," I said. "But this time make it a large one."

FOUR: ROSE

I didn't get to see Marge that night. Michelle wanted to get stuff off her chest and I was on hand to help her do just that. To tell the truth, though, as the evening wore on and the vodka bottles emptied, she seemed more inclined to let her body do the talking.

I didn't mind. I can be flexible.

Revelations come in many forms and in all shapes and sizes in my experience. And conversation can be over-used and over-rated.

I left Michelle Spar's place as the darkness was breaking open. Under the first grey wash of dawn light the weird life TMU had carved out for me felt good.

No. It felt *very* good.

As I climbed into my old jalopy it struck me that I'd been looking at the case all wrong. Thinking that the care agency was a cover for a prostitution racket was just plain lazy. That Michelle and her cohorts were professionals of the late night, red light variety – way too obvious. That it had all gone belly up and they wanted to use me to hang the mayor out to dry – interesting, perhaps, but not good enough to cut the mustard in a Frank Miller mystery. It might have passed the test in those early books, but the readers had moved on. Grown wiser. Wanted more for their money and the investment of their time.

Alice Coor and Michelle Spar were trying too hard. And when people are trying that hard there's usually something wrong. They wanted me to believe that Thomas Jackson was a saint and all they were doing was shoving a big fat rat right under my nose. I couldn't *but* smell it. Bluff? Double, triple bluff?

Michelle was drinking because she was scared. She'd probably been scared for some considerable time, the way she could pack them away; but the amateur, the innocent, was still in there, trying to figure how to get the bottle open. I'd been around long enough to know an old pro when I was in the company of one, and Michelle didn't fit the bill however she was dressed up to look.

And if she was on the game and trying to hide it, why dress the part when the snoop turns up? Same with Alice Coor.

Exercise of mind, body and spirit had worked off the whisky and I drove back along the East Chapel road to my next appointment, with high expectations for company. Michelle had suggested that I visit her supervisor. Rose Morton. And I had seen no good reason to delay the pleasure.

The full glare of morning had risen up fast, and before I knew it I was sitting in the company of Rose Morton, wondering how deep and dirty the well was going to get.

Rose Morton was a few years older than Alice Coor and Michelle Spar and she lived in a tidy little semi befitting her status as supervisor. She shared her life, or at least this particular part of it, with a fireman out beyond where the Estates ended and the East Chapel road turned into the Wilderness Highway. It was upmarket in comparison with the shit hole Estates that housed her juniors, but it was still no place for the faint-hearted.

Unlike the more flamboyant attire of her subordinate Angels, Rose Morton was dressed like a Sunday school teacher with a liking for hand-knitted shawls and long woollen socks. She handed me a mug of something straight out of Alice Coor's recipe book.

"Expecting the same filth you got from the others?" It took me a moment to realise that she wasn't talking about the refreshments. "Tony's home in an hour. That gives us thirty minutes - to be on the safe side."

Her face broke into a grin and then she tilted back her head and laughed like a horse.

"My God," she said, "if you're not all the same. Take a seat."

"I think I missed something," I said, trying to find a way of sitting on the highly polished leather sofa without ending up wearing the contents of the mug I was holding.

She sat opposite me, on an identical sofa, her back to the triple-glazed bay window stacked full of tasteless bone china ornaments.

"You call yourself a detective, but all you're really interested in are the perks along the way."

"You must be reading my diaries. I can't say that I blame you, though. They make good reading and they'll probably publish them all one day."

She curled up her nose like there was a wasp on the end of it.

"Okay," I said. "Humour's a very personal thing, in my opinion."

Rose Morton then decided to cut the small talk and head straight into the heart of the matter.

"Alice Coor's a bigger slag even than Nancy Tate. Slept with her yet?"

"No," I said. "Not yet."

"Her husband's away a lot, so you'll get plenty of opportunity. I suppose you know that much already – if you're any kind of detective. Michelle is a terror for the kiss and tell, by the way. So I know a lot more about you than you realise. Your bedside manner is quite impressive, by all accounts."

I thanked her for the pleasantries. "News travels fast around here."

Rose Morton looked at me with an attitude of pity. Then she stood up, walked to the window, picked up a small china pig and looked out on the garden, all fenced and private and well maintained. "Michelle's a good girl. She doesn't deserve to get hurt."

"Any reason she should get hurt?"

Rose Morton turned back to me. "Every reason. The good ones fall hardest."

I was about to ask which breakfast cereal box she'd taken that one from, when she added, "I know what you're thinking."

"Do you? Even I'm not privileged to that kind of information."

"You think you've stumbled onto a nest of vipers. A coven of witches. So many sluts and only one noble detective to go 'round."

She looked me up and down, like she was thinking of kitting me out with a fresh outfit. Maybe I was due one at that. "I can see how a certain type of woman might find you attractive."

"Care to elaborate on which kind, exactly?"

"The kind lacking any taste whatsoever. Alice and Michelle are good workers, and caring with it. They've known hard times but they're pulling themselves up through hard work and dedication to the ethics of the town council."

I thought she was about to salute.

"Not so long ago you were calling at least one of them a slag."

"And you see a contradiction?"

She put the pig back in the window and sat back down. I couldn't help wondering if her collection of china wasn't a substitute for a real family. I imagined any children coming out of her might look a lot like that ornament.

She looked at me through eyes even colder than those straddling Alice Coor's hooked nose. "So who's dishing up the dirt, then?"

"I take it that's a reference to the death of one of your Angels?"

"Don't play games with me, Mr. Miller. Nancy Tate was bad news but her death had nothing to do with Thomas Jackson."

"So you've heard the rumours, then?"

"You're not funny. Nancy Tate was nothing but trouble and I could have run her down myself the way she treated Michelle. But I didn't, and neither did Thomas Jackson. So I want to know who's stirring things up?"

I shrugged. "I can't imagine."

"Has the name Trudi Tremain come up yet?" she asked.

"I don't believe so. Who is she? No, let me guess: another Chapeltown Angel?"

"Let's say a friend of Nancy Tate and leave it at that, shall we."

"Let's not. She works as an Angel?"

Rose Morton stood up for the last time. Clearly our brief time together was over. The door opened and the bright daylight beckoned.

"Michelle can tell you all you need to know about Trudi Tremain. I wouldn't try to tell you your job, Mr. Miller. But maybe after you've heard what Michelle has to say you should talk to Tremain yourself before you close your file."

"What makes you think I've any intention of closing it?"

"I'd urge you, Mr. Miller, to think long and hard about what you're getting yourself into."

"You make that sound like a threat. And the name's Frank, by the way."

"Good day, Mr. Miller."

The door shut behind me. It was a door that I didn't particularly wish to see re-opened.

FIVE: MICHELLE REVISITED

I called on Michelle Spar for the second time and she had the drinks trolley ready and waiting. This time she wasn't dressed like she was going anywhere and it looked to me like my second session was going to be long and productive, one way or another. One of those detective hunches I get around the right kind of company.

She asked how I'd got on with Rose and I told her. "Like a house on fire." I think it pays to tell the truth once in a while.

"So what brings you back here so soon, Frank?"

I said, "I need to follow up a line of enquiry."

She smiled and I liked it.

"Whisky, Frank?"

"That isn't necessary. On the other hand, yes. Of course."

"Take a seat."

I watched her head for the drinks trolley and wondered whether my enquiries around this Trudi Tremain might wait a little while longer.

With drinks in our hands we talked about Chapeltown without either of us mentioning the fact that it had an elected mayor by the name of Thomas Jackson. And every time she got up to refresh the glasses I thought less about murder and more about the sins carved into me by the sordid hand of my creator.

With a fresh glass in my hand and a proposal forming on my lips, she said, "So what did Rose say to bring you back here, Frank?"

"You think that it was something Rose said?"

She giggled at that and I was about ready to put the proposal out into the stale air of the room when she caught something in my eye.

"Come on, Frank. What did Rose say?"

Hindsight is a wonderful thing. With the gift of it I can see that I should have got the physical side of our relationship out of the way first, playing Frank Miller and being content to do so. It had been enough in the past, chasing dangerous curves around the dirty streets and filthy sheets of this town before caring to make headway in some cheap mystery that this time just happened to involve the Mayor of Chapeltown and his team of *Angels.*

But things were changing, and changing fast.

I said, "I'm interested in Trudi Tremain."

The drink hesitated on Michelle's lips and then she put the glass down. "What did you say?"

"There'll be nobody at the agency I haven't visited by the end of the week, I reckon."

Her smile had left town, taken her giggle with it, and it didn't look like either of them were coming back anytime soon.

"Get out of my flat!"

"Excuse me?"

"You're leaving. Get your coat, if you want it."

"Let me rewind a minute. I say the name *Tremain* and you go ballistic on me. What is it, Michelle?"

"You don't know? You're some detective, aren't you? Door's that way, same as when you came in. You don't need to trouble yourself with goodbyes."

"You think Trudi Tremain started the rumours about Jackson killing Nancy Tate?"

With each mention of the name, Michelle Spar's eyes glowed more fiercely.

"Look," I said. "I've not even met this woman yet. I got her name from Rose Morton. Rose is worried about you. Why?"

"I can take care of myself."

"Can you?"

"I have done up to now."

"Who are you afraid of, Michelle? What's Trudi Tremain done?"

"I said get out!"

I drove towards the Honeywall Flats and all the way I was back to thinking about vice rackets parading as care for the sick and vulnerable. Dark forebodings were crawling all over me and from the confines of my faithful steed I cursed TMU. Had he forgotten the formula? If this was all some kind of a joke then he was overdue some radical surgery on his sense of humour.

I stopped at a garage to buy some flowers for Marge. I needed to see her. It was the oddest thing, but I was feeling guilty about my little liaison with Michelle Spar.

Guilty! Frank Miller!

And as if that wasn't enough of a cross to bear, I was haunted by Marge's notion that I needed to change. Couldn't seem to get the thing out of my head.

I pulled up outside the flats and tried to get my head straight. I gave that up soon enough, deciding that talking things out with Marge was the only way I was going to gain any clarity on the situation.

I lacked the energy for the stone staircase, and instead rode up in the lift. Marge opened the door but didn't look pleased to see me.

"Getting a little bit cold out here," I said. She took the flowers and I started to move through the door.

Until a hand stretched out and stopped me.

"Our date was last night, Frank."

"Look, Marge –"

"No, Frank. You listen to me. You've got to change, and change fast or it'll be too late."

The door closed and I stood the wrong side of it, wondering what to do next. She had been wearing her blue pyjamas, too. I hammered on the door. "Marge! Listen to me, will you?" I could sense that she was on the other side of the door, listening. "We need to talk about this, Marge. We need to get things straightened out."

The door opened. "You're right, Frank. We need to talk. Only not tonight."

She went to close the door but I got my foot in. "Just five minutes, Marge."

"I said not tonight, Frank. Now take your foot out of the way so I can close my door."

"Why did you vote for Thomas Jackson? Why vote for someone nobody ever heard of? It doesn't make sense."

"Your foot, Frank."

"Please, Marge –"

"Come back when you've done some thinking, Frank."

"I've tried that."

"Then try it some more."

I moved my foot out of the way and the door closed in my face.

I walked out of the flats and into the already struggling light. At the right distance I looked back up towards her window. But Marge wasn't there even to see me off the premises. I thought about going back up when she appeared at the window. I waved, and her name involuntarily came out of my mouth, despite the distance between us.

I watched the curtains close.

Why should I care that a woman not right for my world had given me my marching orders? Love 'em and leave 'em, that was the Frank Miller way. Always had been. Let *them* do the soul searching.

This was all upside down and back to front. I should have been out of there like a streak of lightning, seeking out pastures new while Marge lay sobbing her heart out, begging me to go back.   She   was   still talking about change. It was out of the question. Frank Miller didn't change for anybody.

Lights   were   starting   to   come   on   over Chapeltown. TMU was making the days shorter, returning me to where I belonged: beneath a veil of darkness.

For he had created a creature of the night.

I climbed into my jalopy, the moon looking down and laughing. I crossed the city, heading for my hole.

Then I turned off.

I needed answers.

It was time to visit The Man Upstairs.

SIX: A VISIT TO THE MAN UPSTAIRS

First I needed sleep. Even creatures of the night have to find some rest. Sometimes I wished that The Man Upstairs would remember that, though at other times I couldn't really care less.

I drove back to my hole and flopped down on the bed of nails without taking off so much as a shoe.

It was a bad tempered sleep and I woke from it with a sense of relief and a hunger I hadn't felt for some time. I could have killed for bacon and coffee but settled instead for a sink filled with cold water.

Leaving the discomforts of home I made my way to the centre of Chapeltown.

I got out of my old jalopy and stood looking up at the gigantic skyscraper that dominated the central square. The offices were all in darkness, except for the suite right up at the top. There was a light on up there and I wondered if TMU was waiting for me.

For long minutes I stood watching, wondering if a shadow would give him away. Was he planning for this? Was this all part of the grand scheme?

Perhaps Marge had been right after all: perhaps I did need to do some thinking.

As I stood there a feeling of disorientation swept through me. Was this day or night? Was TMU forgetting the basics?

That monstrous building of glass and steel held my maker. The top of it touched the sky and his suite was on the top floor. Day or night he was there; TMU didn't take holidays. Work *was* his holiday.

What kind of thinking would Marge have me do? Thinking of what I had become? What I was in danger of becoming? Were these not questions that only He could answer?

Was that to be my modus operandi now? To ask him about Marge? Ask why he had given her to me, with her incessant drive to change me, if that was not His own plan?

My life, on the rare occasions that I thought about it, was nothing but a series of huge contradictions.

On the one hand I was in charge of my own destiny, figuring things out my own way and taking the consequences for my actions.

Yet on the other hand everything was written for me. All my lines, all my actions. Did choice exist for me in any sense at all, or was it all determined by the great hand in the sky?

Sometimes, in the quiet moments, it would strike me that *that's* what this series was all about. In the old days it was about washing the dirt off the streets. Getting the bad guy and finishing up in the arms of some piece of temporary warmth.

But on days like these...I wasn't sure. Wasn't certain about anything.

I stood there, letting it all flow through me, rooted, on the corner of Soul and Divine, looking up at the Tower of Babel with its dotted windows, some lit now, but most remaining in darkness. This was no-man's land, the place of in-betweens. Yet at the same time slap bang in the centre of everything.

For a few moments I felt the old familiar weight bearing down like it wanted to crush me out of existence. And then I took the crooked staircase straight to the top.

On the top floor only silence greeted me. There was a door and it was open.

"Anyone home?"

Of course he was home. He never left.

I walked in to find nothing but an empty office. Again I addressed the silence.

Again I received no reply for my efforts.

On this floor, at least, one door always led to another. They appeared to be endless. I went through the deserted labyrinth until I reached the inner-sanctum. The engine room. The altar of possibilities. I had been there once before, during the case that changed everything.

The case of *The Black Widow*.

...After the revelations about who I was and what I was I made the journey to find out that God really did exist, and I never needed to make it again. Once I had the faith; once I had drank from the cup of knowledge, I had no reason to do so a second time. Faith ought to last a lifetime - even the lifetime of one kept alive by ink instead of blood...

That's how he wrote it and that's what the public read. Then as now I entered the forbidden realm intending to do nothing but confront him. What happened that first time was this: exactly *nothing*. He didn't show up - though I sensed his presence.

I searched through his papers, feeling his invisible eyes burning holes through me, and found nothing. Then I left with nothing - nothing but the dawning knowledge that whatever existence I had been given, I was stuck with it. There was not a damned thing I could do. The series would go on and I would live between the pages of his books and that was that.

If that's 'faith' then, yes, I found faith that day. And never questioned it. Because the life I had was good. The best. Yet here I was, back again, my faith shattered by an elected mayor, a bunch of crazy care workers and a head full of blue pyjamas.

I was in the playroom, where all things were made. All my old cases tidily filed in every kind of order. I had a sudden urge for nostalgia, to leaf through those days of past glory. To relive the golden years.

The Miller years.

The phrase appealed, and I thought of jotting it down so that TMU himself could see it when he came back from sleeping or whatever else he called this wanton abandonment of duty. He needed reminding of *The Miller Years*. Needed reminding about just what he had created, what he had set in motion, so that he could get back to work and stop messing around with care-worker cat-fights and girls-next-door romance.

On the desk, next to a computer, was a folder. A black folder. I picked it up and extracted from it a document containing the details of this latest case.

'*The Mayor of Chapeltown*', read the legend. Not a bad title, I thought. Yet why did Chapeltown need a mayor, elected or otherwise? It had managed long enough without one.

I lifted the legend and nothing but literary sketches greeted me; trifles of information and background detail. Names that I knew, places I had already visited; but nothing that untangled anything or told me where I was going or how it was all going to end up.

The name 'Trudi Tremain' had been underlined and marked with asterisks, and there was an arrow pointing to it linking it with my own name. Perhaps TMU *was* approaching things from a new direction,

45

experimenting, trying things out and shaking up the formula.

Whatever he was doing I didn't like it. It smelt like change. Frank Miller was Frank Miller and his readers loved him for that. They knew where they stood and so did I. TMU knew that, so why the need to experiment?

On a scrap of paper clipped to the back of the page that linked Trudi Tremain's name to mine, was a four line poem:

> *The Mayor of Chapeltown*
> *How did he win?*
> *Seduced the women*
> *And frightened the men*

I didn't think it was the best thing TMU had ever written. I closed the file and went back to look through the older cases, re-acquainting myself with a couple of favourite endings that almost had me brushing away a tear. Then I heard footsteps.

I prepared to meet my maker.

I watched the door. Waited for it to open. Gritted my teeth and felt my hands form into the shape of fists. I could stand my ground and demand – demand what? – knowledge? - my hour of revelation? Oh, I'd come armed with those intentions on my one previous visit during the days of *The Black Widow.*

And left empty handed as I was destined to do again.

After all, how could I stand face to face with the one who had made this town – the one who had made *me*? When it came to it, I could more easily fly out into the night through the top-floor window than stand eye to eye and toe to toe with The Man Upstairs.

The handle on the door moved…and then stopped. The sound of footsteps receding.

Had *he* no stomach for it, either?

Quietly I slipped away. And didn't look back.

I went back to my hole just for the pleasure of spending a few more hours tossing and turning in my pit. It hadn't all been in vain though. I now had a few more fragments of useless information for company.

There was no point denying it: I had been nothing but relieved when I'd heard those footsteps receding. Was the truth that I couldn't face him? That I was ashamed?

Ashamed of what?

Ashamed of what I had become?

Or of what I was at risk of becoming?

Ashamed of the old Frank Miller?

Or ashamed at the prospect of a new Frank?

Was this the beginnings of madness – and if so was it his madness or mine?

Had TMU given me Marge because he wanted me to change?

Change into what?

Or was it merely a test? To see how far Frank Miller could be pressed without cracking?

At some point I dragged myself through the motions of a shower and then I threw in a shave for good measure. With all of this accomplished I set out to meet a new day.

And Trudi Tremain.

SEVEN: TRUDI

Trudi Tremain lived with her mother. They shared a small house on the west side of Chapeltown, with a small Methodist church behind them and the sinister grin from the Town Hall just about visible from the front window.

Her mother answered the door. She looked a beady-eyed old stick, a little stooped and a touch limpy, though generally intact.

"Trudi's popped out to get me something from the chemist," she said, inviting me through and even making me a hot drink without asking if I was thirsty.

We made ourselves comfortable around the tiny kitchen table. The table looked new, and I wondered if that was why we were sitting around it and not making use of the cosy looking upholsteries in the adjoining living room.

"Nice table," I said at last, smoothing my hand over the teak finish. "Had it long?"

She eyed me like I had asked to see which pillow she was hiding the family savings under.

"Fond of furniture?" she asked.

I wondered if she thought this was humouring me. I chose not to remind her that it was I who was trying to do the humouring. That it was part of the service.

"Only good furniture," I said.

"I suppose you would call that wise."

Her face twitched and for a moment I thought she was about to break out in great guffaws. If that had been the case, she fought the urge as bravely as an asthmatic choking a sneeze over a cocaine deal.

I'd about exhausted my house-and-its-contents conversation that I saved especially for these kinds of situations, and sipped at the coffee. It was the best I'd tasted in a long time and my preoccupation with it returned the conversational initiative to the host.

"Shouldn't be long now," she said, eyeing the kitchen wall clock. "She's a good girl is my Trudi."

I nodded. It seemed a better option than talking.

"I'll say this for Trudi, she would never see her mum go without. Doesn't matter what time of day it is or what the weather's doing. She'd go out and she'd get it – if it was needed, you understand."

I thought I did. At least I wasn't about to ask for an explanation. Involuntarily I found my hand running once again over the table's smoothness.

"You're certainly taken with that table."

"It's a fine table," I said, before I could stop myself.

Her eyes narrowed and I thought I saw something of a fairy tale witch hiding behind them. Perhaps she kept the carved up corpses of nosy detectives in the little room under the stairs. Or else peopled her slaughter room with those who took an unhealthy interest in her kitchen furniture.

Or her daughter.

I heard the key turn in the front door and the old lady sighed with relief in harmony with my own.

"I'm home, Mum."

"That's my Trudi," said the old lady, proudly.

I felt like running my hand over the table one more time for good measure. I stopped myself in the nick of time. The old lady caught my eye. She'd seen what I had been about to do.

The silence grew and as it did so my hands itched. She was watching me. She was waiting for me to do it. *Go on, punk. Touch that table one more time...*

Our eyes locked and the seconds ticked like an unexploded bomb. Then I heard the joyous sound of an Angel's footsteps. A Chapeltown Angel. I wondered how this one might compare to the others.

I caught the old lady, her face like a sunrise, gazing longingly into the open space of the kitchen doorway. She either loved her daughter more profoundly than any god ever loved its creation, or else she was mightily relieved to be no longer alone with a strange man who couldn't keep his hands off the furniture.

Trudi Tremain walked into the room and I stood up. She was clearly surprised to find a strange man in her kitchen, but there was something else going on too. She knew me. Knew who I was, at least. I held out a hand. "Frank Miller," I said.

She fumbled a hand into mine though it took her a few beats to ask who I was and what I wanted. If I hadn't known better I'd have said that Trudi Tremain was at least half expecting me, though perhaps not on that particular day.

"I'm a detective," I said.

"Not been a naughty girl, have you?" asked her mother.

"Routine enquiries," I said.

I could see that Trudi was feeling a little compromised in her mother's presence, and so I took my place back at the table and waited to see how she would get rid of the old stick.

I listened as she told the saga of her trip to the local chemist to get her mother's creams and tablets and everything else that an old lady could possibly need from the high street. I heard all about the queues, the mistakes, the rocketing prices; about this brand against that one and that one against this. I never imagined that stuff could be so absorbing. And there was still the amusing tale about the mislabelled lotion to come.

As Trudi Tremain painted the scene I could see every character in it, and I breathed every line of dialogue with them. By the end of the tale I knew that chemist store, and it was a place of wonder and amazement, where daily miracles sprang from the very brickwork.

"He's taken quite a shine to our table," said the old lady, finally satisfied that she had been told everything about her daughter's visit to the pharmacy; and I could have kicked her shins mightily beneath the table and blamed it on epilepsy. Instead I smiled and waited for the ground to give way beneath me so that we could all die together and keep my secret safe.

The chair creaked beneath her as she got up. "I'll go and apply my cream and leave you two in peace," she said. "I imagine that you have a lot to talk about."

She nodded back at me, queerly I thought, as she left the room. And damn it if I didn't almost stroke the table again, not out of spite, but from the need to do something with my fingers.

"Another drink?" asked Trudi.

She had a look in her eye that I could spot three miles away on a clear day. There was nothing innocent about Trudi Tremain, though she contained what hid beneath the surface like a first rate practitioner in the dark arts of deception.

I won't tell you what colour hair, what colour eyes - won't even give you all of that hard-boiled stuff about bodily shapes that you often get from guys like me. Suffice to say that Trudi Tremain was the real thing. The stuff of every Frank Miller mystery, no question about it. No dressed up doll like the others,

51

Coor and Spar; nothing cheap about Trudi, and nothing obvious either – at least to the untrained eye.

TMU was back on form with this one. The way she moved could raise a corpse; the way she came into a room and what she did with that room to change it in a million ways, defied belief. The way she spoke, too. And the words that came out. In those few minutes my eyes were opened.

TMU really was a genius – at least he could be, when his mind was on the game.

Perhaps I'm getting carried away. The romantic in me tearing a muscle to make itself heard above the beating of a cynical heart. Let's just say that Trudi had an innocence about her that was simply too good to be true. A feigned, practiced innocence that hid a deep, deep yearning.

A yearning that I was more than a little keen to explore.

All the way down...

We sat around the kitchen table making some Chapeltown small talk, and she told me how much she loved working for the agency. Made it sound like a holy calling.

I wasn't convinced. Eventually she asked why I wanted to see her. I asked her to take a guess.

"Has this got something to do with my work?"

I suggested that she tell me everything she knew about Nancy Tate and the Mayor of Chapeltown, along with anything else that she felt inclined to mention along the way.

"Are you interviewing all of the Angels?"

"Only those who come recommended. Your supervisor, Rose Morton, thought I should come and see you."

"Did she now?"

"So tell me what you know."

"Okay. I was naïve. New in the job and eager to please. Maybe I wasn't giving out the right signals."

"You're talking about the mayor?"

"I don't think he meant any harm. I think he had a moment of weakness."

I scanned her face with my bullshit detector set on full. I didn't find any.

"He came on to you?" I asked her.

"I think it's all got blown out of proportion."

"Him being the Mayor of Chapeltown, you mean?"

"That's what this is about, isn't it?"

"It could be. So what you're saying is, anybody else would have earned themselves a slap on the jaw and that would have been the end of the matter?"

"Something like that, I suppose, yes."

"You told some of the girls at the agency what happened?"

"I told Alice Coor. I knew I'd made a mistake as soon as I'd opened my mouth. Alice assured me it wasn't my fault. I don't trust her though."

"And how long after this did Nancy get killed?"

"You don't think Nancy died because of something I said to Alice?"

"I'm not saying that. How do you get on with Michelle Spar?"

She looked uncomfortable at the mention of the name. "Not particularly well," she said.

"You two have a history?"

"I don't understand why you're asking?"

"I'm Mr. Curious, that's all. I can see how all this might have led to things being said,

53

misunderstandings, bad feelings – you know the score. It happens."

"I don't know Michelle very well. I've hardly spoken to her, to be honest. Have you visited her?"

"Yes," I said.

Trudi's eyes narrowed. My hand gripped the table.

"Mum was right," she said. "You do like that table."

"It's a fine table. One of the very best, in my humble opinion."

"Did Michelle tell you something?"

"What kind of thing?"

"What do you want from me?"

"The truth. Nothing more than that."

"About the mayor, you mean?"

"Could be. That's what I'm trying to find out. And I'm getting precisely nowhere slowly. So how about you illuminate my darkness. Perhaps you could start by telling me a little more about Thomas Jackson."

When she failed to fill the ensuing silence, I said, "You must have heard the rumours."

"Which rumours? There are so many going around."

"Blackmail?"

"I've heard that one."

"What about murder?"

"That, too, I'm afraid. We're living in difficult times."

She wasn't kidding.

I could hear footsteps above us. Maybe the cream was wearing off. Perhaps it needed re-applying. Or could it be that the old lady wanted to see how I was getting along with the table and did I want to make her an offer on it before I left?

54

"These rumours," I said. "You don't put much store by them?"

"Do you?"

"I don't know what to think."

I heard the toilet flush above us. I said, "Do you think that all of these women were out to make capital from your experience at the hands of a horny old man? And that Nancy Tate's death was an accident hammed up to look like something it isn't?"

The old lady was coming downstairs.

I leaned forward. "It was you, wasn't it?"

"I don't know what you mean."

"You're the *Chapeltown Whisperer*."

"I don't..."

"The anonymous caller."

I watched her flap around for a few moments, like a landed fish gulping for life.

"You called me up, Trudi. You called me up to whisper unpleasantries in my ear. You told me about Nancy Tate and about the Mayor of Chapeltown and you didn't give your name and you didn't leave a forwarding address."

"Look," she said. "You'd better go. I'll call you later."

"Okay," I said, standing up. "Only don't leave it too long or I will have to come back again. And we don't want your mother thinking that you've been misbehaving, do we?"

The old lady reappeared in the doorway and gave me a look that said she was surprised to see me still there.

I thanked them both for their hospitality and left.

.

Standing on the other side of that door I believed in TMU again. It was all clear to me now. He knew me better than I knew myself and always had done. He was a genius of the first order and utterly benign with it.

Yet how had I repaid him?

My lack of faith had taken me to the brink: rebellion against the one who had created me. The one who had given me everything I had or could ever have. The one who had given me *life*.

I made myself a promise: that I would never again question his judgement. I loved him, and he loved me. A case worthy of Frank Miller was up and running and I was on it.

EIGHT: DOWN BY THE RIVER

Trudi was as good as her word and rang me that evening. She even threw in the whisper for old times' sake. She said I should call on her the next day and so that's exactly what I did.

Old Mother Tremain answered the door, asking if I wanted another look at her table. I could have been offended. But this was the woman who had brought Trudi Tremain into the world, and I was prepared to be forgiving.

The old lady didn't hang around for the pleasantries; and soon it was just me and Trudi, looking at each other like a couple of college kids at playtime. Wondering what to do with all of that free time and energy.

Trudi was done up in a yellow dress, with white ribbons in her hair. She was like a flower waiting to be plucked.

"I want to be straight with you, Frank," she said. "I mean about Michelle."

I was feeling the table again.

"I started at the agency around Christmas and got invited to a party. Michelle was there with her husband. Well, they were married at the time, anyway. They hadn't been getting on, according to the other girls."

"Not many secrets in that agency, I imagine."

"You ever worked with a group of women?"

I held up a hand. "I have to caution you there. I work by a strict code of ethics and I will not allow sexism into my place of work on any account, and I am never off duty. In answer to your question, I do work with women, frequently, though generally on an individual basis. Sorry, please go on."

She gave me a look like she was trying to fit me into a frame.

Then she went on.

"Anyway, by all accounts their marriage was falling apart. People at the party were knocking back the drinks. Michelle was half-cut and her husband not far behind. He made a pass. Nothing too heavy, it didn't really bother me. But it bothered Michelle. She was obviously having trouble facing up to what was going on at home and I was just a convenient scapegoat."

"She blamed the break-up of her marriage on you?"

"I was wary of her, and kept my distance. We've never really had anything to do with each other. Was it Michelle gave you my name?"

"Not exactly."

"What's that mean?"

"It means that your name wasn't music to her ears. She didn't like the sound of it and tried to avoid the use of it as far as possible."

"So Michelle didn't give you my name?"

"Like I told you yesterday, it was Rose who suggested I come to visit you."

"That doesn't surprise me."

"Care to elaborate?"

"They're three of a kind. Alice and Michelle are hookers and Rose, well, Rose is effectively their madam. The Chapeltown Angels – I tell you, that agency is nothing but a cover..."

"Cover? For what?"

"You name it."

"I would prefer it if you did. Spell it out for me, Trudi. I can be slow on the uptake for a professional snoop."

"They were set up by Jackson."

"So what games were they playing?"

"If you can think of a vice, they were into it."

"Can you be more specific? Prostitution? Drugs? The slave trade?"

"There was – is – nothing they wouldn't stoop to. No pie that Jackson hasn't got his filthy fat hands into."

I scratched the back of my head for a full half minute. It was a technique straight out of the first chapter of the sleuth's handbook. It all still seemed a little too obvious for one of TMU's tales. But then perhaps all the stuff with Marge, about me having to change – maybe the twists all lay there, and this Jackson case was a mere foil. I sensed that maybe I was being lulled into a false sense of security. That TMU had something more up his sleeve that he was waiting to spring.

I said, "So Nancy Tate was planning – or at least threatening – to expose the agency and blow Jackson's cover?"

"That's what got her killed. He's ruthless, Frank, and so are they. And you haven't heard the half of it yet."

"So why do you suppose Rose Morton gave me your name?"

"I don't know exactly, Frank. But I don't like it."

It was time to give the back of my head another scratching. "I'm confused, Trudi. You see, a minute ago you said that you weren't surprised that Rose gave me your name, and now you're telling me –"

"I don't know what to think, Frank."

"Why did you ring me?"

"I didn't know what else to do. I don't trust the police."

I couldn't blame her for that. It took a very special kind of person to trust them. And they had my pity, those who chose that path.

I said, "Do you think Rose or the others figured out that it was you that got me involved?"

"I'm not sure. Probably. That's what I was afraid might happen. That's why I didn't want to give you my name, or any clues that could lead back to me."

The room fell silent. "You said you haven't told me half of it yet."

"That's right, Frank. But I want to tell you."

I shrugged. "So tell me."

"Not here, Frank. We need to go somewhere."

"Where do you have in mind?"

We headed out to the Chapeltown woods, a deserted part of our world that stands a few miles east of the Tremain house. I parked up and we walked together through fields that I never even knew existed, on towards the woods. She told me it was one of her favourite haunts. I could see how a person like her could easily fall for a place like that. Good place for secrets.

"It's the place I come to sometimes," she said as we entered the woods. "To think and walk away the blues."

She looked at me.

That certain kind of look.

"Let's go all the way - right down to the river," she said.

"You're not going to get that pretty yellow dress of yours dirty," I said.

"I hope not," she replied.

I wasn't convinced.

Down by the river she told me the rest of it. How she'd ended up sleeping with the Mayor of Chapeltown. I could see in her eyes how hard it was to tell it.

She reckoned he'd spiked her drink and the upshot was that she'd spent the entire night in his chambers.

Trudi passed over the physical stuff but told me in some detail about Jackson talking in his sleep.

It seemed a little odd to me that he'd spiked her drink and yet she was the one who was awake, listening to him sleep-talking. Still, I let the thought pass so as not to interrupt the flow.

"At first he just seemed to be muttering about nothing. You know, making noises, the odd random word, but nothing that made any sense. Then he started saying the word Chapeltown over and over, and then he said your name, Frank."

I said, "You think he has a thing about detectives too?"

Trudi wasn't smiling. I felt the chill. "He said your name a few times, Frank, and each time he said it he started getting more agitated."

"I'm the kind you either have a taste for or –"

"His legs were kicking out. He was really going. I sat on the edge of the bed, thinking it was no longer safe lying next to him the way he kept thrashing about. Then he...said something..."

She tailed off.

"What is it, Trudi? What did he say?"

I waited while she gathered herself together.

"He said about killing you, Frank. About killing you and turning Chapeltown into hell."

I was watching her closely. "He actually said that?"

"That's where I got your name, Frank. That's what got me thinking about contacting you."

"So what were you really doing in his bed?"

"Not getting jealous, are you?"

"More what you'd call curious."

"I wanted to know about Nancy."

"So you slept with him to find out?"

"It wasn't like that."

"What was it like?"

Trudi started walking along by the riverbank. I followed her.

"There was a party."

"It sounds like Jackson's fond of parties," I said.

"You're not kidding. Anyway, he'd been drinking quite a bit and he was giving me the eye. I spotted the opportunity to find out some things that were bugging me."

"About what happened to Nancy?"

"Yes."

"So you contrived to get him alone?"

"He thought he was pulling the strings, but it was me. Except that some time later I woke up in his bed realising that I hadn't been the one pulling the strings after all. I'd learned nothing except he was an even bigger skunk than I'd imagined. The truth is, I don't know what he gave me but I couldn't remember a thing about getting into bed with him or what happened next – except some of it was obvious from how I was feeling down there, if you know what I mean."

I knew alright and I didn't like it.

"I thought about breaking something over his fat head. I thought about going to the police. Then I heard him start to mutter and I heard your name and here we are."

She stopped walking, turned around and gave me another of those looks that she seemed to specialise in. The kind I was a sucker for.

"I'm scared."

I put my arms around her and wondered why heaven always had to have a dark cloud hovering above it. Her sobs were eating right through my shirt.

She looked up at me. "What is it?"

"How the hell did Jackson get the job of mayor?"

"They voted for him?"

"Who?"

"The people of Chapeltown."

I took a moment. There had been no looming mayoral election in the last Frank Miller story, or in any of the others in the series for that matter.

"Why would people vote for someone like that?"

"You mean you didn't vote for him? I thought everyone did."

"You voted for Thomas Jackson?"

"Of course I did."

"Why?"

"He promised the world. Don't you remember? And then he showed his true colours. That's why they made up that rhyme."

"What rhyme?"

"Are you kidding me?"

She sang it.

"The Mayor of Chapeltown
How did he win?
Seduced the women
And frightened the men."

I felt the darkness sweep through me. The scrap of paper in TMU's office.

Was TMU in control? Letting his characters take over?

Experimenting again?

Trudi was saying something else, urgently, through the tears that were streaming down her face.

The last thought I had before we started shedding clothes down on the bank of the river was that Frank Miller could never abandon his first duties to a lady in distress.

NINE: TOWN HALL BLUES

That dalliance by the stream, river or whatever TMU calls the trickle of dirty brown that runs through the lesser known heart of Chapeltown, was new territory for me. I know the high rise flats, the estates and the alleyways; my affairs have been conducted between damp walls and less than pristine sheets, and in the smoke-filled huts that some people in this town and city still have the pride to call home.

We got dressed. Trudi had to get ready for work. She'd call me later. At my *office*.

"You've been watching the detectives. You should visit my office and check out the secretary. I live a double life. At the office I turn into one of those detective heroes that they sometimes show late at night on Chapeltown TV. Phillip Marlowe, Sam Spade, you know the types. TMU's favourites."

"TMU?"

"It doesn't matter."

"I've never heard of any of those people."

"Like I say, forget it. They're characters from another world."

"You're funny, Frank, you know that?"

"I know it. Truth is, my office is temporarily closed. At least, I hope it's temporary. Renovation's the word. So I'm working from home these days, and why I'm not spending more time in bed I can't understand. Except that if you ever spent an hour on the thing I have to call my bed, then maybe you would understand."

"It's because you're spending more time outdoors, getting back to nature."

"Is that what they're calling it now?"

She finished getting dressed. I watched her. Then I said, "Bring many of them down here?"

"What do you take me for, Frank? Can't you tell when a girl's in love?"

"Can any man?"

"Who made you such a cynic?"

"That's a long story."

"I'm listening."

"Let's say…a famous writer that you never heard of."

"I might have."

"Okay then. He's The Man Upstairs, the guy that I mentioned earlier. He writes detective stories about a man just like me. A man who lives right here in Chapeltown. Has a series of his own, too, that people in that other world can't get enough of."

"Are you laughing at me?"

"I've never been more serious in the entirety of my fictional life. As it turns out, this Frank Miller look-alike is on the trail of an evil mayor..."

She pulled my nose. "I'm interested in you, that's all."

"So it would seem."

"Come on Frank - who do you work for, really?"

"Good question."

"You like keeping secrets, don't you?"

"It's not so much a secret, more an enigma."

Her face dropped into a beautiful question mark. I kissed it. "Like I said, I work for The Man Upstairs."

"Upstairs where?"

"You don't need to get into this, believe me."

"But I'm intrigued."

"A guy called Hammett once wrote about a guy called Sam Spade. Then some genius comes along and tries to turn a good idea into Sam Spudkins. But to get all the references you have to believe in a world outside of Chapeltown, where Salvation Army rags exist alongside golden age detectives. A mad world, Trudi, and I mean it when I say that you really don't want to know."

"I think I know crazy when I see it, Frank."

"Oh, believe me, it's a lot worse than that." I kissed her again. "Call me at home. I'm planning on spending some time there. Might even start typing up my memoirs and give TMU a break."

She started doing the kissing, undoing buttons again. Afterwards she cursed me, said I was making her late. Then she got out her mobile and rang the agency. After making her excuses she snapped the thing shut. "You haven't got one of these?"

"I don't like them. I suppose TMU is going to issue me with one eventually, though - to keep me updated."

She laughed again and I liked it. It was medicine for the soul.

"There's something very old-fashioned about you, Frank."

"Is that a compliment?"

"You're different. It's like you're from another time and place."

"I'm strictly Chapeltown, born and bred in the here and now. But you still don't know the half of it."

"I want to know, Frank. I want to know everything about you."

"You're late for work and I've got things to do."

"Like what?"

"Like finding out some more about the Mayor of Chapeltown."

"Perhaps I shouldn't have told you."

"Perhaps you shouldn't. Perhaps what a man says in his sleep should forever remain a secret. But you did tell me."

"Tell *me* one thing, Frank."

"What kind of thing?"

"Anything."

"That yellow dress of yours is going to need a good soaking."

"Tell me something else."

"Okay, you asked for it. The world won't damn well stand still for five minutes. It changes for the hell of it, to keep itself from going crazy."

She whistled. "You should write that down."

"Believe me," I said. "Somebody already has."

We went back to my car and I drove her home. On the way she asked if I was intending to visit Thomas Jackson. I said that I wasn't exactly sure what I was planning to do. That it all sounded more police than PI to me.

Except that the police were a lot worse than useless and were on no account to be trusted with anything more serious than asking directions and giving drunks a place for the night.

"Are you going to follow me?"

We were pulling up outside her house. I saw the curtains twitch inside. I said, "Follow you? Do you want me to? Just so you can tell the girls at the agency that you've had a detective on your back."

She slapped my arm. "Come in for a coffee while I get changed. Then I'll promise to drive slowly so you won't risk losing me."

While Trudi was upstairs getting ready, her mother came and joined me in the kitchen. She didn't miss

68

much, old widow Tremain. She gave me a two minute history of the family, and how tough it had been bringing up a girl in Chapeltown after her husband had gone down a mine one morning and returned to ground level in a man-sized bag.

"This family's seen enough hard times. We're due a break."

It sounded to me like a warning.

Trudi came into the kitchen and then we left in our separate cars, heading in the same direction across town. Every fifteen seconds she checked her mirror, to see that it was really happening. A real detective following her.

I had to smile. Frank Miller, a *real detective*. Look, no strings. Not a wooden boy, but a *real* boy.

I wondered if TMU was listening, but what did I care, really? The girl in the car in front was playing lovers games, acting out fantasies, hers and mine. Whatever life was, it was good to be in it, even this cheap imitation of it.

Looping back around the one-way we passed the Town Hall and I felt its sombre gravity bearing down. The good feelings didn't come back until we had driven clear of those long shadows, and when we finally emerged it was like passing out from beneath a storm cloud and finding the sun again.

The agency building was a couple of miles out of town and looked like something transported from the history books in TMU's world. He referenced his own world shamelessly sometimes, particularly in the later books. It was something the critics picked up on, though opinions were largely divided on how well he pulled it off. He had a thing about Eastern Europe in the days of the Berlin Wall, and if I'm remembering it right, all that was missing was some barbed wire and a few machine guns.

Trudi was impressively discreet getting out of her car, pretending I wasn't there; but I could tell it was killing her all the same. I parked a little way up the road and decided to pitch in for a little while. See if any familiar faces turned up. I didn't have to wait long.

No sooner had Trudi walked into the office than Rose Morton walked out. I figured that the giant monstrosity, that humourless grey-blocked monolith, was not big enough to house the two of them.

Rose drove away from the small car park and I thought about tailing her. But then Michelle Spar turned up and I waited. I was some way from the entrance that Trudi used, and fairly confident that Michelle wouldn't remember my car. What she'd seen of it, if anything, had been in darkness and through a haze of vodka and high emotion.

And dirty net curtains.

Trudi came out. I wondered if they would be better sorting out a rota, preventing them running the risk of bumping into each other. Perhaps the comings and goings reflected the work they were doing and not the clashing of personalities.

She got into her car and nodded towards me as she pulled off. It crossed my mind to follow; see what her day looked like. Then Michelle came back out. I was bent on following somebody now that Trudi had given me the taste for it. And I hadn't anything else planned, except maybe dropping by the Town Hall later to see how our elected friend was settling in.

I had a hunch Michelle Spar might have a similar plan before the day was done.

Her first call was a mile south down the road. A two bedroomed council house. She stayed about twenty minutes, then came out, climbed back in her car and headed back. She made half a dozen calls in a couple of hours, all council properties, always using a key-safe to enter. I jotted down the addresses, pondering what kind of service constituted care in the community these days.

She was heading into the centre of town, the Methodist church coming up, the Town Hall to the left. She parked up and I followed on foot as she entered the ugly gothic construction that housed the mayor and the rest of Chapeltown's chosen.

People were starting to head home. There was a sense of moving against the tide as I followed Michelle Spar through the outer corridors of the vast maze that housed just about everything you could ever ask for in the name of local power and bureaucracy. I saw her swipe a card at a barrier and watched a set of doors swing open. I didn't have one of those cards.

She disappeared down the corridor beyond the glass doors, and as she went I wondered what might have become of the two of us had the name Trudi Tremain not come into the room as we sipped on our respective poisons.

A middle aged man was walking towards the glass door. I fumbled at my pockets, looking flustered, consulting my watch. In respect of my artistry, he promptly used his card and the doors opened.

"Mayor still down there?" I asked, moving through the doors ahead of him.

"Should think so. Know where you're going?"

"Remind me."

"To the end, turn right, then follow it around, second door on your left."

I scooted along in time to catch the tail end of Michelle disappearing through that very second door left. A cleaning woman appeared along the corridor, coming my way. I gave her my best, my finest Frank Miller grin, and thought something mischievous moved in her eye.

I said, "I'm looking for Mr. Big."

She giggled. "Aren't we all."

I conspired with the joker, using up more laughter than her humour deserved before making my demand for payment. I pointed a casual thumb toward the door through which Michelle had disappeared. "I'm looking for the mayor."

She looked me up and down. "Are you authorised?"

I flashed my ID card, too fast for her to see what she was looking at.

"Through there's his lordship's chambers. If the meeting's cleared he'll be in one of the room's leading off, and no doubt getting juiced on honest tax-payers money."

"I thought we'd elected a man of the highest integrity," I said.

"So did I."

"So what happened?"

"Give a man some power," she said.

"You think power's his undoing?"

"Either that or he fooled us from the start. Either way we're stuck with it."

She looked around, as though acutely aware that she was talking out of turn to a stranger. I thought of that stuff TMU was into. The Berlin Wall. *1984*. All that totalitarian bullshit that was making him paranoid - and that kept creeping into his later books. It wasn't healthy. He could get obsessive about stuff like that sometimes.

The cleaning woman seemed to be suffering from a similar bout of paranoia. Maybe it was the books she was reading – or maybe it was the place she was working. In an attempt to put her at ease I thanked her for her honesty, put a finger to my lips and winked. She giggled, then covered her mouth. Cute didn't come into it.

I wished her a good life. A long and happy one. And then I slipped in through the door.

The main chamber was circular, and the empty chairs, in mild disarray, seemed to suggest, for some reason, that a lot of uninteresting people who loved the sound of their own voices had left for the day, possibly to gloat over the importance of their existence and the contribution that their lives and work made to the people of Chapeltown in particular and the world in general.

TMU was putting thoughts into my head again.

I focused. A dozen rooms led off the chamber. Did I feel lucky?

I didn't feel lucky. And what if Michelle emerged from one of those rooms and found me here? I thought about the rhyme written on a scrap of paper in TMU's office, and repeated by Trudi down by the river.

The mayor. Seducing the women and frightening the men. Taking Chapeltown to hell.

Did I know enough to be playing it the hard way already?

Answer: *No way.*

Did I know what exactly I was dealing with?

Answer: *No.*

What I was getting into?

Most certainly not.

Was my very presence in the Town Hall putting people at risk?

Very likely.

Putting Trudi at risk?

Almost certainly.

I had a sudden and severe case of the Town Hall Blues.

I turned around.

Frank Miller was leaving the building.

TEN: FALLING IN LOVE BLUES

Night fell over Chapeltown. I was back in my hole and the phone was ringing.

Marge.

I must have sounded cool and she commented on the fact. I made no apologies and she eventually gave up, saying it was like getting blood from a corpse.

I thought she might at least apologise for turning me away.

She didn't.

I got the distinct feeling that the shoe was on the other foot. Maybe if I'd made an effort, played the game and met her half way – but who knows when there's a woman on one end of the line, and on the other…what?: a detective kept alive by a writer obsessed with murder? Thinning out a man's blood until his veins ran as clear as spring rain, only not as pure.

I was a hard-boiled creation and TMU knew it better than anyone. So what was all this falling in love bullshit? I was a heart breaker and they loved me for it. In all the Frank Miller mysteries I had never come close to falling in love. It was never on the agenda. In that respect TMU and Frank Miller were two of a kind. And yet, in this present farce, I had practically settled down into married life with Marge and was getting all boyish about another settling-down type going by the name of Trudi Tremain.

Except that in Trudi's case I couldn't be certain. There was something moving around under the surface of Trudi Tremain that I couldn't make my mind up about.

I sat up a few hours doing nothing but thinking of going to bed. Then the phone rang again and this time it was Trudi. She was almost off her shift and wanted some of Frank's best company. It was a your-place-or-mine scene, and I didn't relish either. My hole was long past serving as suitable accommodation for entertaining young ladies.

Which left her place. With old Mother Tremain listening with a cup to the wall. Could I live with that?

I pondered the question for a good second or maybe even two.

I arranged to meet Trudi at the end of the road. Mother Tremain would be in bed, awaiting the key in the door so she could say goodnight.

And that's the way we played it.

We walked into the house together and two pairs of shoes on the mat most likely sounded exactly the same as one. Trudi shouted up the stairs and the returning voice bounced back down again. And so the subterfuge began and I was buzzing with it.

We spoke in whispers and shared a beer. Trudi said that in the unlikely event of her mother coming downstairs there was usually a three minute warning as she thudded out of bed and scrambled around the bedroom, blinded by the light, trying to find her dressing-gown.

"Sounds like you've done this before."

"Never ask a lady questions like that, Frank."

We started getting a little closer and it wasn't long before interest in the beer, fine though it was, had been replaced with a more urgent calling. Trudi took my hand and led me towards the door. I stopped and she started giggling. "Not shy tonight, are we?"

I pointed my thumb questioningly towards the door, and the staircase behind it.

"Frank, relax, will you. She'll be asleep already."

"How can you be so sure?"

"She has her pills lined up on her bedside table, and when she hears me come in she takes them. Ten minutes later she's gone." She looked at her watch. "I make it almost twenty."

"I didn't realise you ran such a tight ship."

She took my hand again. "Ready?"

"Won't she hear us up there?"

"Have you never done anything like this before? Never broke into the dormitory at the local nursing station?"

I tried my best to look horrified. "As a matter of fact, no," I said. "Have you?"

"Frank, there's a bathroom between our rooms. Unless we start screaming, she won't hear a thing. Anyway, having to contain it makes it all the more exciting, don't you think?"

We walked up the stairs in tandem, Trudi leading the way. Once inside her room she closed the door behind us. I was beginning to wonder if I might die before I got to heaven, every creak sounding loud enough to bring the authorities running or else usher on the fatal stroke.

I heard sounds from the landing. "Listen," I said.

"What is it?" whispered Trudi.

"Nothing."

Another sound issued and I jumped. "Frank, for God's sake - what's the matter with you? Look, if you're not comfortable with the arrangement..."

"Who said I'm not comfortable?"

I let something timeless overcome me, blotting out all other considerations. Trudi was looking full and peachy and I was –"

"Frank!"

"I heard something. I thought she was coming in."

"She has a pee sometimes. She's half unconscious and she isn't going to come to check baby Trudi's sleeping soundly. Now relax or we'll have to call it a night."

I sat there, naked, listening to the bowl filling next door, then footsteps receding. TMU was turning me into a figure of fun. He was destroying what he had once so lovingly created for the sake of a few cheap laughs. He should have known by now that Frank Miller didn't do romantic comedy for anybody, not even for *him*.

I was fast losing the feeling. Then Trudi set to work.

She pulled the covers over the both of us, and cut to the business in hand with a purpose that cannot be praised too highly. Magic of the highest order, raising the ghost of the old Frank Miller, his/my natural-born exuberance riding out, praising existence in the time-honoured fashion.

As we collapsed together in the afterglow, the door opened and the light came on. I looked back over my shoulder to see Mother Tremain's unwelcome face smiling down on my bare hind quarters. "Hello," I said, trying to retain some dignity.

The old lady stood there, blinking, as though she couldn't take it in.

"I think I left some kippers under the grill," she said, her nose twitching.

Then the door closed behind her.

I lay in Trudi's warm embrace. Then, miracle of miracles, I started to laugh. Not the cold, cynical sneer that I had cultivated over twenty previous adventures, but something altogether more radiant and joyful.

"What is it, Frank?"

"Beats me," I said, though I knew well enough.

I was in love again. I had been on the brink of rebellion. About to raise a fist in the direction of the one pulling my strings. And now I was filled with nothing but forgiveness.

And admiration.

The man was an artist.

And I was hopelessly in love again.

In love with my creator.

In love withTMU.

But love never lasts.

ELEVEN: THE FIRE

In the restless hours I took Trudi to the all-night theatre on Hidden Valley Parade. It was a place TMU had once built for me. A small picture house where I could sit alone and muse on cases that needed cracking; a place to brood on scores that needed settling and graves that needed filling. Nobody else in Chapeltown seemed to know about that fine little palace, yet they ran films there every night of the year.

The film was tame, which was strange for that place, though I couldn't fault the company. Sitting there in the dark, Trudi munching on popcorn, the two of us swigging cokes, I could almost swear to feeling seventeen again.

Except I'd never had the pleasure the first time around.

TMU hadn't blessed me with youth; he had brought me into his Chapeltown world at an age sour enough to match my vocation. That age was never stated, and it had given rise to some confusion amongst fans of the series. In a recent book TMU had described me as being on the wrong side of thirty but still clear of the shadows of forty. Some eagle-eyed readers had noted that TMU had used a very similar line in the very first Miller Mystery. TMU had commented, in a rare interview, that he liked to insert small errors from time to time to give those inclined that way something to do at conventions.

I digress.

When the film was over Trudi dragged me into an Indian restaurant that I didn't know existed. It seemed that this town was full of surprises - and just when I'd started to believe that it could show me nothing new.

I told her straight. "We're still in Chapeltown and I'm still Frank Miller. I've drunk pop with you tonight but there are limits. People will talk. I have a reputation to uphold and this particular engine runs on junk food and whisky. I need you to swear an oath of discretion."

All she did was laugh, call me crazy and force curry down me in an effort to convert me. Fantasy land receded as the real world of business and other people crept in like so many thieves upon our tiny Shangri-La. Friction at work was getting to her. Michelle and the gang were turning up the heat.

"Have any of them made specific threats?"

"Nothing you could nail down. Vibes more than anything. But I'm not paranoid, Frank. I know what's going down."

"Do you?"

"I can handle it. Are you still on the case? Is this business or pleasure now?"

I tried to look hurt, though the feeling was genuine enough. I'm not sure how well it came off. Sometimes acting's a sight easier than real life, and sometimes it isn't. Trouble being I was no longer sure if I was acting or playing it straight. I opened my mouth and trusted to blind luck that something constructive would come out.

I said, "I'm here because I like the company."

"Sorry," she said and kissed me.

I got some more drinks. We clinked glasses and I said, "Why don't you change agencies?"

"Jobs aren't easy to come by these days. I'd need a reference, and a good one at that. I doubt I'd get one from Rose Morton."

"What about a different line of work?"

81

"This is what I know, Frank. Anyway, why should I let some sad bitches screw my career? I've done nothing wrong and they can't get rid of me that easily."

"They could set you up."

"Maybe they will. I wouldn't put it past them. This isn't my first agency; I know how to look after myself."

"Maybe Nancy Tate thought she could handle it, too."

"She didn't have you, Frank."

"Is that why I'm here? The bodyguard picking up a few perks along the way?"

"That's a horrible thing to say."

"Only if it's not true."

She seemed about to cry. I kept watching. The tears didn't fall. At last she said,

"What are you thinking, Frank?"

I said, "I'm thinking that you're afraid."

"I'm no threat. I don't need keeping quiet."

"Do they know that?"

"I don't regret coming to you."

"I don't regret it either. But I'm digging in their world and they're naturally inclined to want to know who released the dogs. I'm doing all I can to tread carefully, Trudi, but I can't guarantee they won't put two and two together."

"I'm not scared, Frank. Do what you have to, and don't hold back on my account."

We clinked glasses again and drank to that.

With the sunrise we went back to her house against my muted protests and better wishes. On the way she convinced me again that her mother wouldn't know anything about the antics of earlier, not with all of that medication inside her.

Somewhere up above I could hear the distant peals of laughter. TMU didn't think a teenage hard-on was enough; he was going all-out for short-trousered schoolboy guilt, with matron jokes written across his face in pimples.

We went through to the kitchen and guess who was sitting there? It was like old times. I was back at my beloved table, feeling the wood while Trudi made a round of hot drinks. The old lady smiled at me, and I was looking for some clue that might foreshadow the dressing down I imagined was coming.

I tried not to blush.

We got back onto the major conversational topic: the table. She seemed to find my manner "highly amusing" and I was getting used to being the source of laughter. As we sipped our coffees the three of us small-talked like we had been a family all our lives. It was as painless as having a tooth drilled after a heavy dose of anaesthetic, but it still left the feeling that there was something better I could be doing.

At last the old stick started yawning, really sucking the air. I wondered how anybody that tired could sit upright. When she still didn't move I took my cue to leave.

Trudi showed me to the door. She had the day off and promised that if I would be a good boy and let her catch up on some sleep, she would reward my thoughtfulness. "Let's make it midnight, Frank. Whistle three times beneath my window and I'll be waiting."

Later, sitting in my hole, looking forward to another night of subterfuge, and reminding myself how whisky tasted on an empty stomach, I watched an envelope fall through my letter box. I hadn't had that happen in quite a while.

The envelope looked impressive, and the letter-headed missive inside equally so, with its council emblem proclaiming good things for the people it reckoned to serve.

Underneath was a brief type-written message.

THE GATES OF HELL ARE OPENING.
SEE YOU THERE, FRANK.

The love letter was signed,

Thomas Jackson, Elected Mayor of Chapeltown.

I blinked and the message changed into some dull invitation to visit the mayor in his chambers. A circular distributed to every resident of Chapeltown.

I screwed it up and went to bed.

I woke up in time for the midnight hour.

My radio alarm – given to me in the course of my last mystery by a blonde with legs that stretched all the way to heaven, but who had, it must be said, a limited concept of the trimmings and trappings of a golden age, hardboiled detective – eased me from my slumbers with some swamp blues.

My dreams had been Trudi-this-and-Trudi-that.

Love sick Frank, raring to go.

My plan was to try to convince Trudi to take some time off, and bunker down in some safe place where the dark angels of this town couldn't find her. Then I was going to visit Thomas Jackson and make my own mind up about what was going on in Chapeltown.

It seemed a good plan. Get Trudi out of harm's way and then bust the case wide open and see what spilled out.

As I was about to leave my hole I went to switch off the radio.

The news came on.

There had been a fatal fire in a two-bedroom house close to the Town Hall.

Two women had been in the property, mother and daughter.

Both had perished in the inferno.

TWELVE: CHAPELTOWN LIBRARY

There was another letter on the mat.

YOU SHOULDN'T BELIEVE EVERYTHING YOU'RE TOLD BY KISS AND TELL GOSSIPS WHO KNOW NOTHING ABOUT THE REAL WORLD.

Again it was signed,

Thomas Jackson, Elected Mayor of Chapeltown.

The police weren't treating the fire as suspicious. Why didn't that surprise me?

The way they drew up the scene before they closed their files was something like: the old woman's corpse was found in bed, and her daughter's in the same room. The old woman had taken strong medication, and too much of it. The daughter had been trying to rouse her and left it too late to get herself downstairs and out of the property. There were no phones upstairs and anyway the fire had been too intense. Emergency services couldn't have done much even had a call come through. The fire had started in the kitchen.

Constructing the scene from evidence available, money was on the old woman coming downstairs in the night to make a drink. A milk saucepan had dried and caught fire, the old woman back in bed and still orbiting planet Pharmaceutical.

The coroner suggested that, with the amount of medication inside her, it was amazing that she'd made it down the stairs at all, let alone back up. His conclusion: that she had been in a state of less than full consciousness and very probably sleep walking.

A tragic accident wiping two innocent lives from the Chapeltown register.

That was the official verdict. No mention of how much poorer Chapeltown had suddenly become. I had a thirst to make more disturbing connections. The urge to find somebody to hang it on became my constant companion.

Somewhere in that raging void Marge called me. Nothing heavy, just wondering what I was up to. She'd heard about the fire and wasn't it appalling that something like that could happen to two innocent people. She'd read that the young woman was a care worker who was also looking after her ageing mother. That by all accounts she was a dedicated young woman, sacrificing a social life to extend what she did for a living into what remained of her time, using her professional skills to minister to the needs of a sick parent.

I'd read those accounts myself. Hearing them again, innocently expressed by Marge, was breaking my heart.

"You don't sound yourself, Frank."

"I've been better, I'll admit."

"Maybe you need to take some time off."

Oh, I'd been thinking about it.

"You know where I am, Frank."

I knew where she was. And I also knew that I wasn't the right kind of company. I was nothing but a drowning shadow, summoning whatever was needed to revisit TMU and blow this hidden iceberg out of the water.

I went along to the funeral service and hung around at the back of the chapel. I saw them come in: Rose Morton, Michelle Spar, Alice Coor and one or two

87

other women, all from the agency by the look of them. Colleagues come to pay last respects to their tragic comrade and the mother she doted on.

The priest hammered it up, too. He might even have used the phrase "modern-day Florence Nightingale" at some point. My mind kept drifting. I was looking at the back of the heads of those other *agency angels* and wondering, just wondering. Then a phrase, or a tune would snatch me out of it and the sense of loss would burst back over me. I wondered what had come to Chapeltown. What sickness.

I left before the end. I'd seen and heard enough. And when I left I was thinking about Marge. Uncharacteristic thoughts. Thoughts out of season. Thoughts that didn't belong in my world. Thoughts that belonged inside the heads of younger heroes who still believed in love and romance. I steered the thoughts back into some kind of selfish logic. Of what would become of me if anything happened to her. And then the thoughts turned around, with no interference from me: *what would become of Marge if anything happened to old Frank?*

I didn't like that way of thinking. It had always been a full time job looking out for myself. I didn't need the baggage of looking out for somebody else.

I knew that everything was changing.

That everything had already changed.

That time had become infinitely precious.

Life too.

It was like infinity itself was coming to an end. The essence of life – even a life as unreal as mine – no longer lay in cheap thrills and cute endings.

I needed to lie down.

In the midst of all of that bleakness, I went to the central library in Chapeltown. There was a hankering inside me to search out every one of TMU's books and tear them up, page by page. They might still survive in his world, but here they could burn.

I had never been inside that building before and so I asked at the counter for assistance in finding the books that I wanted to destroy. The assistant asked for the name of the author and when I told him "TMU" he looked blank and then showed me how to use the computer. I tried putting in 'The Man Upstairs' but all the files came back empty. I messed about on that machine until I was ready to throw it out the window.

Then I had a stroke of inspiration.

Or egomania.

I typed in the name Frank Miller. A series of options came up. Maybe I was on to something.

Somebody was coughing in my ear and wouldn't you know it: one of the staff chubbing about would I need the computer much longer. Apparently there were other customers queuing behind me and I wondered if they fancied burning some books too. I asked for a few minutes longer and my wish was ungraciously granted.

Then I turned back to the terminal and found what I was looking for.

The celebrated cases, all of them; nothing missing at all. The good times, the glory days – all there in black and white.

I took the reference number and moved into the part of the library that contained the books. It was vast. Rooms within rooms. I felt like I was in a little row boat on a rolling ocean, and I rowed through those libraries within libraries until at last I happened upon one small room. A room drowning in books.

I went in.

On the shelf facing me I found them. The Chapeltown copies of the *Frank Miller Mysteries*. Every case I had ever worked.

I was a child at last, and the man in the red suit had just disappeared back up the chimney. There, left in his wake, everything I ever dreamed and found to be real. Not a return to childhood but my first taste of it.

I took them down from the shelf, one by one. At first I could hardly bear to touch them, as though they might crumble to dust and be gone forever. But when this didn't happen, I became bolder, and in no time I was rifling through them, chewing my fingers as I read through one passage, roaring with laughter over another.

The greatest moments of my life.

All the moments of my life.

Whatever I had come here to do, it would be left undone. I wouldn't be destroying the writings of TMU, rather I would be tearing up the life of Frank Miller.

I put the books back as the black cloud of rage descended. In that moment my impotence was legion. I blamed TMU - and I blamed him for everything. Why wouldn't I? It was his universe. We were his creations, after all. Who else could take the blame?

I wondered if he had ever loved. If there was somebody in *his* life so that I, like Frankenstein's monster, could confront him and rip the heart from his bride on *his* wedding night.

A flash of lightning split the inside of my skull. I remembered something, half remembered it, yet couldn't bring it into focus. I ran my finger across the spines of the books and took down *The Black Widow*.

The case where everything went wrong - and then right again. The case that showed me hell so that I would come back, reborn, not as the man I was, but transformed, knowing my true nature and at last believing in *God*.

And there, at the heart of the book, I found it. The turning point of the entire series. The moment when I found out who I was and what I am. What TMU had created.

The real Frank Miller, for better or worse.

I could hear the footsteps of the assistant approaching, as he came to inform me that the library was closing.

THIRTEEN: THE DYING MAN

Those past cases, looking so important and real bound up on that library shelf, must have done something to my mind. Reading about the glory days, re-living them - it was a wake-up call.

A call to arms.

I'd been sleeping on the job for years, living and breathing on auto-pilot. And all the time something had been festering deep down in the bowels of this town and I hadn't seen it.

A new kind of darkness had come to Chapeltown. Something truly monstrous was about to be unleashed. What had happened to Trudi Tremain and her mother was only the beginning.

Trudi had been dead more days than I could count on my fingers, but not so many that I ran out of toes. The police had done their poking and the coroner had done his, and then the priest had laid the whole business to rest.

I was the last person to spend a night in that house, the Tremain house, and live to tell the tale. Yet nobody had come to me to ask what I knew, where I fitted in, or if I could add anything to their reports before they stamped them, put them into triplicate and filed them away where no living soul would have to bother with them again.

The Chapeltown police didn't have the best reputation to begin with; but if the mayor really had the town in his fist then I needed to exercise a little extra caution before I started making wild accusations.

I did some poking around but the work was slow and every hour of every day I wanted to be doing something else. Perhaps a couple of weeks selling rotten fruit off the market; or a month behind a bar, catching up on the small talk that happens in the watering holes of Chapeltown when the invisible children that exist only in rumours are long tucked up in their beds for the night, or else should be.

Few hours passed when I didn't find Trudi's face plastered on the inside of my head. And then the swell of anger and the thirst for justice would sweep over me like a raving thunder cloud, with pretensions of turning into a hurricane, leaving me no choice but to disbelieve in the possibilities of sheer misfortune and cry out for blood and pain.

TMU's favourite words were 'WHAT IF.' All his best ideas began like that.

So 'What If ' Trudi was right and the mayor really was planning to take Chapeltown to hell? What had Trudi known? Or what did they *think* she had known? Trudi opened her mouth and Nancy Tate died. I start asking questions and then Trudi and her mum are dead too.

What if the gates of hell really were starting to open?

What if The Mayor of Chapeltown was opening them?

What if I was losing the plot?
What if TMU was losing it..?

I did some tailing, mainly women from the agency. Maybe if I played it patiently, at a distance, something might turn up that would get my nose twitching. Some stroke of dumb luck, most likely – that's the way it generally went.

During the glory days I had been a well-oiled machine – and I'm not just talking about the beer and whisky. In those days I would pick a case to pieces, never making a wrong move, waking in the middle of the night with blinding insights that would lead me into a delicious denouement, arriving always in the nick of time for the final turning of the screw.

It got so that I could practically do it in my sleep.

And maybe that's the paradox. I was so damned good at it – and TMU was so damned good at making me so damned good at it – that the thing grew stale. The challenge had gone out of it.

So then TMU saw fit to give me different work and different working practices, and the strangeness of existence deepened. But you can only paint moustaches on the Mona Lisa for so long – and that's another of TMU's favourite lines and it's cropped up a few times along the way.

Yet the point remains: How long would the Frank Miller of old have tailed around the streets of Chapeltown, watching care agency workers disappear into the houses of the sick? Was TMU, desperate for new ideas, moving into territories where Frank simply didn't belong? Was TMU not just giving old Mona something to decorate her top lip, but throwing in the full beard and mutton-chop sideboards to boot?

One day I followed Michelle Spar from one of her visits, and watched her park up close to the Town Hall. I tethered my rusting heap, but this time I didn't make a ham-fisted attempt to follow her into the building. I sat it out. I didn't have to sit it out for long.

It was late in the afternoon, and she seemed pleased about something as she climbed back into her car. When she pulled away I followed her. Maybe she was thinking about the steak she was having for tea. Or the vodka evening ahead.

Or the death of Trudi Tremain...

She drove to the house of Alice Coor, and stayed no more than a few minutes. Then the two women came out together, getting into Michelle's car. I followed them to Rose Morton's house.

It was gripping stuff.

It was well into the evening when the three emerged from Rose Morton's house, getting into Michelle's car. I followed them back to the agency. Then I waited another hour. When they came out the three had become four, though I didn't recognise the fourth woman.

It was closing on midnight when the crew parked up back at the Town Hall. I watched them get out of the car and head inside. When they failed to return to the car after an hour I thought about going in. I was getting sick of all this nothing. Wondering why TMU couldn't let me sleep instead of riffing around trying to make something happen. Forgetting that his first duty was to entertain. Forgetting that there were readers out there.

The women came out of the Town Hall and I noticed how fresh and laundered they looked, like they'd showered and touched up the war paint. Naturally I wondered what they'd done to get dirty in the first place.

I watched them get back in the car. They were bursting with something, but trying to contain it until they were off the street. Then I saw something erupting inside the car, a mixture of laughter and elation. I guessed that the business, whatever it was, had been concluded for the night, short of Michelle Spar dropping them back at their respective homes.

I finally called it a night. How long could I keep this up?

I was bursting to do *something.*

What kind of waking up was this? I'd had busier times sleeping.

The next day I was back outside the agency, looking for the one amongst them that I hadn't had the pleasure of visiting yet. It took me almost the entire day, but she had to go home sometime. I was following right behind when she did.

I watched her go inside a small, terraced house on the edge of town, a little way short of the Estates. She let herself in and closed the curtains. I kept watch for a little while.

It looked like the neighbours one side were away, whilst those on the other side, at least those sitting in the doorway, or lying out in the street, or making faces at the window, were too out of it to notice anything unless it could be played loud enough to wake the dead.

I drove home.

I was back early the next day and only had to put in an hour before the mystery girl was out of the house and pulling away in her car. One set of neighbours hadn't returned from wherever they'd gone, and the others were spilling in and out, some wearing headsets, others moving to the sounds that blasted out into the street every time the front door opened.

The front door to the house that the mystery girl had just left looked flimsy enough to take the old Miller card trick, so I stepped boldly up and knocked. When nobody answered I gave it the standard count. The card was already in my hand and when you slipped it hard enough, and at the right angle, a certain type of door imitated the sound of a certain type of lock snapping back, and I was inside with the door closed behind me

96

before the neighbours could even have worked out what song was playing.

It had been a while since I'd got my hands dirty, and good dishonest labour was bringing me the feeling that the Frank of old was back on the rise. I looked around the downstairs of the property, making sure of my escape route out the back should the situation require it. Nothing but the flotsam and jetsam of a working life greeted me and I could feel the satisfaction seeping away.

I decided to take a quick look upstairs.

There were two bedrooms and a bathroom. I checked the smaller bedroom first. There wasn't much of anything, not even a bed. I nudged open the door to the other bedroom.

Two eyes greeted me.

I stepped back onto the landing, feeling the air whistling out of my lungs. A man, pale and emaciated was hugging a bed sheet up around his neck. "Who are you? What do you want?"

"It's okay," I said. "I was looking for your daughter?"

"I haven't a daughter."

"Your care worker then."

"Who?"

"The lady who was here earlier."

"Jan, you mean? Who are you?"

"Jan, that's her."

"What do you want with Jan?"

I said, "Can I get you anything? Jan's popped out for a while."

He glanced nervously at the empty side of the bed, then back at me. I didn't like it. He had to be ninety. Jan – thirty, maybe younger. It was a double bed and he was only using one side of it. I was trying not to dwell on the possibilities.

"Any idea what time she's coming back?"

"Who are you?"

"I'm from the agency."

"What agency?"

"The care agency that Jan works for."

I watched him.

While he watched me.

"*What agency*?"

He could be mad.

Or maybe just insane.

He could have lost his mind and that was why this angel of mercy – this Chapletown Angel - was visiting.

But why was she spending the night with him? Or at least part of it? Was it all more innocent than that? Had I spent too much time living in the sick imagination of The Man Upstairs?

"So tell me," I said. "What exactly does Jan do for you?"

His eyes grew so big that I thought they were going to burst out of their cracked and oozing sockets. His tongue circled dry lips, his cheeks stretching his mouth into a gut-churning grin. "Do for me? Wouldn't you like to know?"

I felt the heaves starting.

"Wouldn't see a soul if it wasn't for Jan."

"Is this your house?"

"All I've got left. No money, no nothing. Jan, that's all. And she can have this place, bless her, because she's the only one of the stinking lot who cares. Doctor gave me a fortnight tops. I've had a week of it already. Without Jan these past couple of nights I don't know how I would have coped. She's not like the other girls they sent."

"I bet she isn't."

"What's that?"

"Good, is she?"

"The others did what they could for me, but they sent Jan when they knew I was on the way out. They give you special favours to ease you through it. I tell you, I used to be the first to knock the public services - but I didn't know the truth of it."

He wasn't alone in his ignorance.

This mayor of ours was nothing if not radical.

"Puts a different kind of light on it, doesn't it?"

"On what?"

"Public service."

"Are you trying to mock me? Do you think it's clever to taunt a dying old man? If you were in my position, wouldn't you be getting what you can before the curtain comes down?"

He was making an effort to rise from his bed. His face was purpling and I didn't much like the look of it. "Hey," I said. "Take it easy."

"If you report her – I'll kill you. I'll come back and fucking kill you."

I was holding up both hands. "Your secret's safe with me, old timer. Save your heart attack for Jan." I backed into the doorway. "She's coming back later?"

"What business is it of yours? Who are you?"

"Just a concerned citizen. Listen, can I get you anything before I go?"

"Just fuck off, will you. Jan's all I need now. And I'm telling you, if you try to ruin anything, I'll haunt you, God help me."

"I'm going."

"You're not a supervisor? Who shall I say called?"

"The student."

"You look too old. And too stupid."

"I'm exploring my options. Giving this racket a try. Government's retraining the workforce and I'm thinking of trying care work. This visit's helping me to decide if it's the career for me. To tell you the truth, I think it might be too demanding. Times have changed from when my grandmother was in the business. You need a stronger stomach these days. She was right though."

"About what?"

"She reckoned that you can't take it with you. Spend it while you can, that's what she told me. Whatever it's costing you, old man, it's got to be worth it."

"Have you finished?"

"Get some rest. I'll see myself out."

"How did you get in?"

"Agency key, one size fits all. See you on the other side."

"And tell those bastards to keep the music down!"

I made my way downstairs and showed myself to the door. I had the urge to return to my hole and take a long hot shower.

And then I was going back to visit TMU.

FOURTEEN: AN INVITATION

I went to the Tower of Babel he called home and took that old crooked staircase again, straight up to the top. And then I turned the place upside down. And when I found nothing I did the same again. Maybe by the time I'd finished it was back the right way again.

Time passed and I can't say how much of it. But at some point I came across a drawer that for some reason I hadn't noticed before. A drawer tucked inside one of the desks. It had the word MYSTERY written across it.

Inside was a bundle of papers. I could tell they were recent.

I was shaking reading through those pages, and still shaking when I reached the last one. The clichés were welling up inside me, but I resisted them, every one of them. I put the papers on the desk and sat down.

Wasn't *he* a man of surprises?

TMU planning a murder.

Plotting a murder.

Something I hadn't bargained for.

Yet why not? This happened every day of my life. This is what he did and where I fitted in. TMU never stopped thinking up ways to kill. TMU had built his empire on his secret skill as a murderer on a serial scale.

So why did it seem so shocking to me now?

The act of discovery?

The falling into place of the obvious?

There was a deeper level operating - and something lurking down there in the shadows. Something hideous – and it was waiting for me.

TMU hadn't done anything to surprise me since the days of *The Black Widow*. Nothing even remotely original. Instead he had remained content to let all his new ideas become old, and then knock those old ideas around until the kingdom came and the kingdom went, riffing ad nauseam.

And I had been content to let him.

Was he waking up again?

Was I?

A weird buzz stirred inside me. Excitement blazing the highway of my bones. What was unfolding here might turn out to be his grandest design. His masterpiece.

Our masterpiece.

I placed the papers back inside the drawer, not even attempting to make the office appear undisturbed. When he 'woke up' he would know anyway, because keeping secrets from TMU was not a possibility and it never had been.

If he was taking me to another level then I wanted him to know that I was ready and waiting for whatever he'd got.

I left him to it.

That evening the case took off.

I'd returned to my hole to drink firewater, my mind working itself into a knot over the contents of the secret drawer. The phone rang. A man's voice I didn't recognise was giving me directions and expecting me to be there.

I told the man that I had to stay in and clean out my underwear cupboard, and to try me again in the spring.

He didn't laugh. Told me I ought to be there. It was a threat, no doubt about it, but he made it sound more like an invitation that I couldn't refuse.

"I like your sense of occasion," I said. "Okay, you have a date. What would you like me to wear?"

The line went dead.

I arrived at the Town Hall, its carnival grin greeting me like a long-lost friend. My car door opened without any help from me. I had thought the car park, and the streets that fed off it, deserted. The figure opening my door appeared out of nowhere, and didn't say much, didn't say anything. Just walked and I followed, half a step behind.

He used a swipe-card to open the side door, and the same card opened a further series of doors as we moved in a subtle downward spiral. I asked him if this was the way to the centre of the Earth, but his answer was predictable and consistent and he didn't even have to part his lips to give it. More doors opened and closed, only the clip-clop of our shoes breaking the dead-silence of the endless corridors.

I said, "You people never heard of golfing carts?"

He didn't laugh. Why should he? We kept on walking. After a while I asked him if he knew any good jokes. When he didn't answer, I asked if he knew any bad ones. He wasn't discriminating: he didn't know anything.

So we kept on walking and then at last we stopped. He opened a door, one that didn't need a card. It didn't surprise me. Any soul planning a raid on this place would have given up a mile back.

There was a small reception area, and at the counter a lady with long hair was standing there, smiling. It was the kind of smile that some people can keep up for hours at a stretch.

I heard the door close behind me. I turned around and the man was gone. The sound of a heavy key turning suggested it would be no good trying to open that door without assistance of some kind.

Besides, the woman was showing me that she could do more than smile, beckoning me with beguiling eyes. What could I do? I had nothing else planned for the rest of that evening.

"Just the two of us, then," I said.

She offered to take my coat. I emptied it of my car keys and a few bank notes and handed it to her. "No offence," I said. "I had a rough upbringing."

She checked the pockets. "Lost something?" I asked her.

"No phones allowed in this club."

"Sounds like my kind of club, then."

She eyed me as though I were a specimen arriving from a distant world. The smile had left along with the beguiling look. In their place I could find nothing but mildly disguised contempt mixed with just a soupcon of impatience.

"Search me," I said. "I'm the last man in the universe without a mobile phone. I thought you'd brought me here to force me to wear one."

No, my jokes were not getting through, and I asked if humour had been banned altogether now from the civic offices. (They'd been threatening it for a good while.) She didn't laugh at that, either, though she did search me. I didn't attempt to conceal any enjoyment.

Convinced at last that I was not armed with ring tones, she led me through reception, along a short carpeted corridor, stopping outside a black door with a key waiting in the lock. She opened up and invited me to step across the threshold.

I was looking in on a small, intimately furnished room consisting of a woman sitting on a single bed, two chairs and not much else. Music was coming from somewhere, and in the absence of any visible sound system I assumed that it was being piped in. I'd done this scene in my time, strictly in the line of duty, of course, and this was nothing to write home about. But the woman sitting on the bed was – depending on who was at home opening the mail.

I stepped inside and heard the door close behind me, the key turning.

I said, "Looks like *you're* stuck with me now."

She smiled, every bit as professionally as her colleague had done once, and invited me to sit down. While she was getting busy making me comfortable I asked how much all of this generous hospitality was costing the tax-payers of Chapeltown.

"You don't have to worry about that," she said. "Not tonight."

"Just thinking ahead," I said as she eased off my boots. "I hate surprises, particularly in the morning. I mean to say, don't think me presumptuous, but I take it we'll be going the distance. After all that walking to get here – I think it would be rude not to offer the weary traveller a bed for the night."

"Just relax and enjoy."

"I'll do my best. I will certainly do that. You know, I hadn't realised the council had branched out so far. Not so very long ago it was a job and a half getting them to empty a bin. I'd have to call that progress."

She turned away, taking something from underneath the pillow. It was some kind of mask and she began strapping it to her face. "Whoa, steady there," I said. "Frank Miller is as broad-minded as

105

anyone, but during the week he's strictly a 'fish and chips supper' kind of guy."

She turned around and some of my forebodings eased. As masks go it wasn't so bad, and I could see that cartoon cat-women might have much to offer a punter busy losing touch with reality.

"Okay," I said. "Peas at the weekend, but that's my limit."

I started to ask some questions along the lines of why the town council saw fit to entertain its residents in such fashion, but the company was bent on distracting me and soon I decided that asking questions was an over-rated pastime, even for a detective.

We got up to some tricks though I still wasn't certain what the mask accomplished. At some point another girl came in, but my powers of observation were mysteriously diminishing and I couldn't even have said what colour her hair or anything else was with any degree of confidence. At some stage there were three of them, then four. We did a lot of things, some peculiar and some I wouldn't be proud to recall. I was surprising myself with every hour that passed and not entirely ruling out the possibility that I was in the throes of a whisky induced coma.

My eyes opened. The two chairs had gone. They hadn't been needed as far as I could recall. The women were gone too. I was in a room with a bed and nothing else, deep in the bowels of the Town Hall. If my mind had not been playing tricks, I had been treated to a night of remarkable excess, some of which I could remember vividly and some – the later developments in particular – remaining merely as images seen through a bowl of over-rich soup.

My coat was back with me, on a hanger over the door handle. The rest of my clothes were back on, and a quick inventory revealed that I had not been robbed of my few bank notes or car keys.

I was thinking about heading back through to reception and asking if they did coffee. I tried to stand up but my legs gave way, leaving me in a heap on the floor. After some considerable effort I made it back onto the bed and didn't try to do anything else until the world had finished spinning and I knew which was the ceiling again and which hand was holding nine fingers and which the talking rabbit.

Then the far wall started to move. I rubbed at my eyes and watched the wall develop a crack down the middle, the two parts moving away from the centre, revealing a screen.

It looked to me like it was movie time.

Then the show started. The room on the screen looking suspiciously like the room I was already in. And the actors none other than the girl in the cat mask and me.

It was going to be just like old times.

I tried to tell the unseen operator, "If you're going to just show re-runs, I'll skip it and go on home." But my tongue felt loose and shivery inside my mouth, and the words echoed around my head in a manner suggesting they couldn't find the way out.

The screen was showing things I didn't care to see, focusing less on her and more on the parts of old Frankie that I don't believe were designed for the silver screen. And these were no edited highlights. They were screening the entire night in real time.

It got worse, and then it got a lot worse.

There were six women in all sharing that screen with me, all of them wearing masks.

Through the thick fog on the inside of my head, the mask at last made sense. They'd been piping something more than music into that room, and they'd kept it steady all night long. The vaguer memories of my evening became sordid realities. I knew the camera was capable of lying, yet these images came with a ring of truth.

As the ringing got louder I would have traded every good memory from the Frank Miller vaults for the belief that all of these skeletons were really hanging in some other sucker's closet.

The film progressed and I witnessed events of which I had no memory at all. By the time the shameful episode involving the fourth woman kicked in, the film had ceased being merely a tasteless fantasy, descending rapidly towards the downright disturbing.

Could I physically have done that?

Could she?

The fifth woman was not only performing the unspeakable, she was the recipient of acts to which I could never sanely lay claim. The soundtrack alone could have closed down a city. By the time the sixth masked vixen hit the screen, my hands were double-jointing to cover my eyes and my ears, and I was trying to make the numb fish swimming about in my mouth conform to the actions of screaming.

But nothing was coming out. My face appeared in close-up, the features distorting in slow motion, my mouth making the shape of the scream; and then, as though an invisible wall of glass had shattered, I heard, in surround-sound, the screams finally break into the room.

They were full of damnation and belonged at the end of the world.

I sat in silence as the wall slid back into position. The screen was gone and I thought of the scene in that film from TMU's world – the one where the sea rushed back after the Israelites had passed out of their place of captivity.

But I was still in mine.

Huddled on the bed, I began to feel the intense cold. My arms wrapped around my legs and I squeezed until I couldn't stand the pain.

Then the door opened.

FIFTEEN: THAT OLD CIVIC HOSPITALITY

I watched Michelle Spar walk up to me. She didn't look about to ask if I wanted tea or coffee, and I didn't make any wisecracks about the standard of accommodation.

I saw her hand pull back and still I didn't see it coming.

The stars came out and for good measure she called me a "dirty slut" and a "dirty slag." I felt in no mood to question the difference. After a little more time spent trying her way around the language, she left me with another star-show.

I was alone again, and preferring my own company at that. Then the door opened and in came Rose Morton.

Rose's manner was very different. She sat at the end of the bed and looked at me in a kindly sort of way. I wondered if they were pulling some lousy good-cop/bad-cop routine. She took her time before saying anything. Her voice was soft, mellow even. With my head resting back on the pillow I felt like a child waiting for a bedtime story.

"Frank – it is alright if I call you Frank?"

I nodded. "I've not had the best of nights. You'll have to excuse me if I'm not so chatty today. But yes, Frank's fine."

She smiled, didn't hurry. "Have you any idea what all of this might be about?"

I shook my head. "Council business has always been a mystery to me. How about you?"

"Oh, I know everything and I'm not even a snoop."

"Good for you, it's a lousy job."

"You surprise me."

I shrugged. "Frank knows nothing. He never did and he never will."

"Can I ask a personal question, Frank?"

"Fire away. I have a free morning."

"You spent some time with Trudi Tremain."

"Is that a fact?"

"Did she talk about the care agency she was working for?"

"Not that I recall."

"What about the Town Hall?"

"Again, I don't recall -"

"The mayor? She must have said something about Thomas Jackson."

"Chapeltown has a mayor these days!"

She waved a finger at me, like I was a naughty child giving silly answers. "Oh, Frank," she said. "Hasn't there been enough unpleasantness?"

I nodded. "Very probably, yes."

"Do you expect us – me – to believe that Trudi told you nothing?"

"It wasn't that kind of a relationship."

"What kind was it, Frank?"

"The kind you don't discuss in mixed company."

"I've been watching the little film you made last night, Frank. I don't think you need to be coy with me."

"Impressive, wasn't I?"

She sighed. "You're not making it easy. Perhaps we'll talk later."

She went out and a little time later Michelle Spar came back in. She called me some names and then I had a few more aches and pains that I hadn't noticed earlier. She didn't stay long, but I wasn't sorry to see her go.

Rose Morton was back with the same routine from scratch. It was as though our previous conversation had never happened. After a while I was starting to get tired of my own smart replies and decided to take a nap.

I tried to, anyway. She kept the questions coming, though, despite seeing how tired I was what with all the sex and violence on offer. I couldn't quite catch the tide of sleep, yet I let out a few meaty snores in the hope that she might give up, go away and let me rest.

"Trudi reckoned the mayor has plans to turn Chapeltown into hell."

I felt my eyes inadvertently snap open.

"What's your view on that, Frank?"

"Sounds like the kind of gossip women thrive on. I reckon Nancy Tate had a genuine accident and the gossip-mongers couldn't resist trying to make a story out of it. Case closed."

"So why are you still asking questions, Frank?"

"Am I?"

"It would seem so."

"Perhaps it's because two innocent people died in a fire and one of them was Trudi Tremain."

"How do you know she was innocent?"

"Let's look at it the other way around: what was she guilty of?"

"Did Trudi ever tell you about her so-called 'encounter' with Thomas Jackson?"

"She didn't mention it. Maybe it didn't happen. Or maybe she was less kiss-and-tell than some of the others. Or maybe she did mention it. So what? I can't see that it matters. What matters is that she was murdered in cold blood."

"Hardly cold, Frank. I hear that place went up like..."

She grinned. I tried to raise a fist but my energy levels were below those of your average dead man. I collapsed back on the bed. Her face loomed over mine. "Don't play games with me, Frank. Somebody wanted you to look into Nancy Tate's death, and then you heard Trudi's silly schoolgirl rumour."

"You don't believe that."

"Don't believe what, Frank? I can see the little cogs whirring around in your head but you're not making any sense."

"How could I? The man writing my lines has lost his mojo – and I'm wondering if he'll ever get it back."

Her expression formed into the shape of a perfect question mark. I couldn't resist.

"The same deranged lunatic who's shuffling me around the page is filling your head with crazy notions too. The Man Upstairs – you should check him out."

"Poor Frank. What have they done to you?"

"So Trudi died because she asked me to look into Nancy Tate's death? What's the official line?"

"Officially it's a shame."

"That's it?"

"These things happen. It's an uncertain world we live in. Even in a little town like ours, terrible things happen."

"Sounds like you're threatening me."

"See how things can be misinterpreted? I think we'll leave it there for now."

"Are you sending Michelle back in? I think there are a couple of places she missed."

Rose winked at me. "I should try to get some rest, Frank. I think you're in for a long day."

The door closed and I embraced unconsciousness.

I woke up, Michelle Spar standing over me. The side of my face was stinging. I would have preferred a coffee. I decided not to say what was on my mind.

Her face changed. The iron growl subsided and a seducer's pout replaced it. She started taking her clothes off. A fictional lifetime ago this might have been a welcome development, but at that point I wasn't exactly feeling in *that* kind of a mood.

Michelle started doing a dance that I didn't recognise, and she was moving well. I felt inclined to put a fist through her face, though a part of me was having other ideas. It was then I realised that I was naked again.

Me, Michelle and a bed. Both of us full of hatred. Both needing the release of violence.

I understood my thirst for retribution, but still couldn't get my head around hers. She was dancing over me when I said, "You still sore at me seeing Trudi?"

That earned me a slap across the face. To tell the truth I was getting a little sick of slaps across the face.

"Don't," she said, hovering above me, fists clenched, "ever mention that whore's name again in my company, do you hear?"

"You had them killed? A woman scorned?"

"I'll show you a woman scorned."

"I've seen it. I'm watching the movie. They even gave me a part in it."

She was still working on her moves, coming close, backing off. "The girls thought you were quite impressive."

114

"Where'd you learn to dance like that?"

She knelt down on the bed and straddled me, her tongue licking around the bruising on the side of my face. "That whore and her old woman were all wrong for you, Frank."

I'd never done it before, and I hated myself for doing it then. I made a fist and silently dedicated the move to Trudi and her mum before letting it go, straight into Michelle's dirty mouth.

She fell back off the bed and landed on the floor, holding her face like a trained footballer. My knuckles were throbbing from the blow and a part of me, deep in the guts, seemed aglow while the rest remained wretched. She got up from the floor, evidently in pain, though there was some satisfaction going on that the blood couldn't hide. She nodded to me and left the room.

I waited, alone, wondering what came next. *Who* came next. What and why, pain or pleasure?

I heard the far wall moving and looked to see the screen emerging once again from the middle of it. I was looking at two actors, both amateurs: Frank Miller and Michelle Spar. She was straddling me, whispering something into my ear that I couldn't catch, though I still retain the despicable memory of it. My fist was forming, my arm pulling back, the splintering impact nicely done, Michelle arcing through the air in slow motion, the blood, the close up of my face, displaying a brief second of satisfaction, falling quickly into shock and disbelief and repugnance.

The scene was instantly repeated, this time dwelling on the blow, long still frames of my flicker of joy, then the blood, then the whole thing repeated, over and over, until I was begging for them to take it away and put on some cartoons.

115

The next time I woke up I was fully clothed except for my trusty PI coat. It had served me through seasons of glory. I told myself that it might do again. In any event I wanted it back.

Rose Morton came in and I never got to asking her about my coat, my head too full of more trivial matters.

"Frank, a lot of people were impressed with the earlier scenes in your movie, but they were a little disturbed by some of your later work. People are suggesting that you've blown your image, possibly forever. I mean, how can you treat your audience that way and expect them to give freely of their time to come and see you?"

I was beginning to think that my wisecracking days were over. If all this was designed to break me, then I had to hand it to them: these guys were professionals.

"I can see," she said, "that you have a question. Make it a wise one this time."

"Why are you going to all this trouble?"

"Trouble? Frank, you amaze me. How long have you been in the gumshoe trade?"

"You wouldn't go to all this trouble if you were just planning to…dispose of me."

Her laughter sounded practically good-natured. "What makes you so sure? A girl's got to have fun, you know."

"Torturing me for kicks? I don't think so."

Her eyebrows lifted up a good inch either side. "You don't know women, Frank, or men either for that matter."

"I know Michelle has a score to settle."

"You think Michelle has a grudge because you left her for Trudi Tremain?"

"Left her!"

"Didn't you?"

"I was doing my job -"

"And that includes trying to get inside every woman that you interview in the course of your…*enquiries?*"

"Who are you – the sex police? I mentioned Trudi's name and Michelle ordered me out of her home. I didn't know Trudi at that point. What the hell -?"

She waved a finger. "If you're going to raise your voice, I will have to leave you alone again. We're making progress, let's not spoil it, eh? Look, Frank. If that's all it was - a grudge - wouldn't that mean all of this was Michelle's arrangement and all for the sake of a petty jealousy - doesn't make a lot of sense, does it?"

"None of this does."

"You don't know the fuller picture, that's all."

"I know it has to do with Jackson."

"Do you?"

"Did Jackson have Nancy killed? Did he have Trudi and her mother killed?"

She sucked the air in between clenched teeth. "Big questions, Frank."

"But I'm not getting *big* answers."

The room fell into a metallic silence. Rose Morton glowered down at me. "The things you did to those women – the sheer depravity. And after that, Michelle comes to see you and you punch her in the face. A man punches a woman so hard in the face that you can practically hear her teeth falling like nine-pins - are you proud, Frank? Can you imagine what people are saying about you – the kind of man they are taking you

117

for? How can you continue to work in this town? How can you even contemplate living in this town?

"Do you really think that a town this size can keep a secret so big? Do you, Frank? Do you still believe that, or do we have to convince you some more?"

Her eyes were blazing.

I waited for them to cool.

When they didn't I said, "Let me get this straight: You're telling me to leave town. If I open my mouth you'll use these films to discredit me?"

She put a finger to her right temple and thought for a moment. "Is your credit good in this town, Frank? You've been around a long time. That alone should count for something. Depends what you find yourself up against, though, doesn't it? And these things, once you get into them, they're so, oh, what's the word…?"

"The only words I can think of are blackmail, vice and corruption."

"That's some vocabulary for a small town dick."

"Oh, I don't know. In this kind of company they roll off the tongue. You're using the camera to blackmail me into keeping my mouth shut. You don't want me blowing the whistle on all that nice vice and corruption you've got going with Mr. Jackson and the gang."

"So why go to all this trouble and expense, Frank? There are easier ways than this to keep a man quiet."

"So you win. I can't figure it. You want me alive to find out what I know, that much I can figure. But why look at keeping me ticking in the long term when you're holding all the cards?"

"You saying you'd prefer it if we put you out of your misery?"

"I'm saying you've no reason to use a camera to keep me quiet. Like you said, there's easier ways."

She shook her head and laughed. "People go in and out of favour. Nothing stays the same very long. One day Frank has no coinage, and he goes into exile. But change comes along, and one day the town that forgot Frank wants to remember him again. Wants to hear his story. He has coinage again, and boy does he want to use it."

She looked at me and frowned. "Something puzzling you?"

"Just that I haven't the damndest clue what you're talking about."

She moved to the door. "I think we'll leave it there, Frank. You must be tired."

Sometime later the door opened again and Alice Coor was standing above me. She looked as hard as a rock and then as soft as the mush my brain was slowly turning into.

"Remember me?" she said. "We have some unfinished business, I believe."

"You're the angel sent to kill me with kindness."

"Ironic, isn't it?"

"I thought I'd tried everything, but ironic sex is definitely a new experience for me. Not sure I'll be recommending it, though."

"You've still got quite a few new experiences coming your way, Frank, so just shut your mouth and take it, eh?"

She was undressing and I watched the scene with the bored fascination of a man who has been overly-indulged. She joined me on the bed and I had not the strength or the will to fight any more battles.

119

What was one more fierce onslaught performed on weak flesh? I was in the capable hands of highly trained professionals, and council operatives to boot. If satisfaction was not guaranteed I could ask for a complaints form at reception on my way out.

I was laughing and she asked if something was funny. I shook my head and laughed all the louder. I had no doubt that it would all be filmed and shown back to me until I finally dissolved into full-time madness.

Could be that the secret to all this was aversion therapy: the whole shooting-match nothing more than somebody's idea of rehabilitation.

TMU?

Setting all this up to teach me a lesson?

A plot to change me?

Teach me for snooping around in his office; teach me for discovering the hidden drawer; take me up a gear, beyond the constraints of the genre he had chosen for me?

I felt my pulse quicken.

Alice Coor was setting to work, and going about it with a vengeance. She was good, despite my distracted mind. Imaginative, too. While Coor put me through my paces I thought about how far TMU would go. It might turn out that my uncovering of his plot to murder some as yet undisclosed victim hadn't been one of my smartest moves.

The full power of the thought took hold as Alice Coor began to moan out the beginnings of some bastardised lover's lament that she'd no doubt learned from a dark angel's evil twin on a night-trip to the lake of brimstone.

I followed suit, like the gentleman I am, and joined in with the sick chorus. It was worse than any fist in the chops – or anywhere else, for that matter. But it passed the time.

When the door closed I lay sweating in the darkness. There was a longing inside me that was declaring all out war. It came upon me like a cloud of spirits and it burrowed down deeper than a heartbeat.

I could see Marge, see her like she was standing over me. Longing, in the *Gospel according to Frank Miller*, had always been about the flesh, the blood, the whisky and the retribution.

Everything was changing.
Frank Miller was changing.

SIXTEEN: ENTER THE MAYOR OF CHAPELTOWN

My thoughts had taken on a dreaming quality; I didn't know how far I could trust them. Perhaps the city fathers would send me from here a fully certified madman. Howling and drooling; incarcerated for the rest of my days in some unlovable institution, telling them nightly that I was not mad. That I had a tale to tell.

And that would be my lot: screaming out tales of sinister care agencies and the improbable secret life of the Mayor of Chapeltown until my lungs were raw and my night sedation arrived in buckets.

Or else I would leave this place to live out an existence in muted exile, my tongue as broken as my spirit. Poor Frank. Lost on a battlefield of strangers. One moment raging, full of fight and spleen; the next filled only with fatalistic resignation.

The screen re-appeared.

Main feature: Frank and Alice.

It looked more animated than I remembered. Quite stirring, in fact, the way they'd filmed it. Alice Coor, whatever else could be said about her, was all woman. She had a body that could wrap itself around the most awkward corners of another human form with the ease of a snake. And all the time I had thought myself too distracted to take full account of the inner and outer mysteries of Alice Coor.

Not according to the screen.

Up there I didn't seem distracted at all. Giving Alice my full attention.

The things she was coming out with – I couldn't remember any of that stuff. Could be they'd dubbed a soundtrack. The whole thing looked more like an affair

– a sordid, twisted, gratuitous and brutal one, naturally – rather than a carefully staged show for some sick voyeur's benefit.

When we finished, the scene cut to Coor's husband, home-movie footage of the semi-tamed brute in domestic bliss. Then back to me and Alice Coor. Then another figure, big and bloated.

Thomas Jackson?

Those fat eyes had mayor written all over them.

I sat up. He was looking right into me. For a moment I thought that the screen had vanished; that he was there in the room.

Then it was back to me and Alice Coor. Then footage of Mr. Coor amid the comforts and discomforts of home. Back to the mayor - staring, accusing; sitting in silent judgement. Coor on top of Frank, the camera angled from somewhere down amongst the tangle of our feet, her behind filling the screen, then the angle shifting, the camera bringing my face into focus.

Then another change of angle, giving the illusion that I was watching all of this unfolding through the lens. Alice Coor slowing. The image of her husband looking down on the scene, standing large, and then turning away. Another figure taking his place, arms folded across an official chest, serious and solemn, a piece of black material draped across his head like an old-time hanging judge.

Fat eyes glowing.

A final twist of perspective and I was looking down on Alice Coor's hide as it ground to a halt – the conduit bringing me face to face at last with Thomas Jackson.

Porn trash or art house, I would prefer to leave that to higher authorities to decide.

The screen froze on that final, eternal image, before fading to black. Yet even when it was gone, it was still there, blazing behind my eyeballs, imprinted on the inside of my head for all time. An image that I will never be free of - branded into the brain for all eternity.

Framed perfectly between the cinematic cheeks of Alice Coor's arse –

-    The Mayor of Chapeltown.

SEVENTEEN: CHECKING OUT

I lay in the darkness and all I could see were Jackson's eyes, burning out of the blackness. I felt the mythical beast rise up; the thing I'd often heard of but never had the pleasure of: that iron face of nightmare inviting itself to bless me with my inaugural taste of *fear*.

I lay alone with that foreign emotion for company as the hours rolled as slowly as weeks. Somewhere in that ocean of time I found sleep. It was a lonesome journey, stinking and vicious; and in its depths – call it a dream, call it awakening – I glimpsed some truth.

I woke up fast. I woke up knowing that the moment was upon me. Either I succumbed to the vagaries of oblivion or else I took matters into my own hands, for better or for worse.

My clothes had been conveniently laid at the foot of the bed and I wasted no time getting into them. Then I went over to the door and hammered on it. "Okay," I shouted. "Where's the eggs and bacon. The lab rat has woken up."

I tried the door and to my surprise it opened. In fact it opened so easily that in the effort of pulling at it with such – as it turned out - unnecessary force I almost fell back onto the bed.

The corridor outside was empty. I set off back through the labyrinth, the way I had come so many uncounted hours and days before.

There was not a soul around – just the feeling that I was being watched for company. Maybe my movements were being shown up on that screen in my old room. Perhaps they'd be showing it again later.

Perhaps, if it made general release, I could catch it at my leisure at the picture house in town.

The glass doors appeared ahead of me. No guards, no gangsters in hats bearing automatic weapons, just the mundane signs of ordinary life - people milling about in the daily grind, coming and going and making no difference to anything but not hurting anybody either.

The glass doors opened and I kept on going. Nobody seemed to notice me. I went through the next set of doors and then, in the distance, I saw daylight.

I stopped walking. It wasn't enough to say that this was too easy. TMU would never let me have it *this* easy.

And neither would Thomas Jackson.

I didn't like it.

Still people were coming and going, crossing my path from every direction. Still none of them were taking any notice.

I felt at my chin, expecting to find enough stubble to sand down a wheel-arch; but it was clean. I looked down at my clothes, and they didn't appear at all ruffled or stained. Catching my reflection in the final set of glass doors I'd expected an abused tramp looking for a warm place to squat for the night. Instead I was greeted by a Frank Miller that I recognised, and looking every bit as ready for business as the turbo-charged butterflies who flew past like summer was dying and it all had to make sense before nightfall.

I had to be crazy.

Crazy or else still asleep and dreaming.

I shook my head at no-one, for no-one. TMU was crazy, not me. TMU was busy with his first draft again, trying out this, messing with that.

And he was messing with my patience, too.

From now on my moves would be my own.

I concentrated until I could almost feel the blood coming out of my forehead. Trying to be sure that I was doing the deciding, not carrying out the wishes of some 'higher' presence.

I made to step forward and stopped, at the last possible second, attempted to fool myself, in a controlled fashion, not letting on that I was about to step or not step, cough or not cough. A woman was walking past, minding her business, and I wanted to make a grab for her, like Frank never would have done. I watched her come past, my hands moving behind me. I was looking right at her, like I meant to do it. Then, at the last moment, I ducked out.

She sensed something, though, and who wouldn't. I saw the eyeball twitch and the peripheral vision working overtime.

I watched her go, saw her turn around and maybe she muttered "jerk" or maybe I was mistaken. I can't say that I would have blamed her either way. I looked back towards the daylight, before turning my gaze towards the ornate roof above me. On the cusp of freedom I addressed my fallen god. "Frank's checking out of this insane mystery for a while. You still plan to screw-up what you created – well, over my dead body, pal. Now there's a thought for you."

I walked on towards the light, still soliloquising as I went. "You created me and I'm your responsibility. And I'm the greatest thing you ever did. You *want* me off the case? What kind of life's left for you without Frank Miller?"

The light was getting stronger. The cracker-barrel philosopher within getting wiser.

"Think you could make it without me – you don't get that lucky twice. I live forever, mister, and

127

that's something you should consider. You need advice on how to see out your time? Listen, you come to me, you couldn't do better."

I stopped talking, looked around. People coming, people going. None of them taking a blind bit of notice. "Bit players," I said, under my breath. "You never did know how to paint in the little people."

I walked out into sweet daylight. I had been a creature of the darkness for too long.

As my feet hit the street I tensed. Where was the turnaround? Nothing was ever this easy.

I stood and watched.

Waited.

Nothing.

Had Thomas Jackson done with me? Did he really believe that the footage he'd taken of me in compromising situations with the Chapeltown Angels would keep my mouth shut? Was there a subtle warning that Marge would follow in the manner of Nancy Tate and Trudi Tremain if I opened my mouth or moved against Jackson?

The minutes ticked by and still there was no rough greeting, no sign of anything to disturb the surface movements of inconsequentiality that went on around the civic offices of Chapeltown every working day of the week.

I found my car and it didn't even have a parking ticket. I wanted to feel lucky about that, but something inside was bent on denying me. My old jalopy started first time though I wasn't sure where I wanted it to take me. A part of me wanted to see Marge, but only a small part. If there was a cloud full of trouble about to fall from the apparently clear blue sky, I didn't want an innocent like her standing anywhere near me. There'd been enough grief on my account already.

There, I've said it, though I'm not particularly proud. The sentimentality done and dusted.

I was on a mission to change and yet at the same time I wanted some of the old Frank Miller back. I had an urge to find a face that I could sink a fist in, and all the way up to the elbow - and not just once.

I passed the Honeywall Flats and wondered how Marge was passing the days. And though I was sorely tempted, I didn't stop, not until I was pulling up outside my hole. If I was being followed then I didn't want to lead them straight to her. Chivalry – or at least the real kind - had never been my strongest point, but I still had some layers of decency.

Didn't I?

I thought about playing some more games, establishing that I was making the choices and not TMU. Yet the truth was that I had no idea what level of delusion any of us were operating under. And what level of reality. I didn't even know if this very thought was itself a revelation, the manifestation of a higher wisdom, a twinkle of the dim light of victory on a far horizon.

Or else the first signs that I was throwing in the towel.

Or that it was being thrown in for me.

All that stuff was way too deep and to dabble would lead me, I had no doubt, to the straight jacket and the padded cell. I was out of my depth. Better to concern myself with the here and now, the tangible. The stuff that came straight from the guts.

Like the fact that my 'escape' had been hardly an escape at all. More like a set-up. There had to be a turnaround.

If they gave me enough rope they could watch me hanging myself. Or at least watch where I went and who I was talking to.

I got out of the car and crawled into my hole. Was I still prisoner at the Town Hall, waiting for the next reel of the movie to start? About to be awoken with a fist in the chops..?

EIGHTEEN: TMU PLOTS A MURDER

I awoke with a start. A sound outside had cut through my fantasy of playing trampolines on Jackson's bulbous gut. It was good enough fun, don't get me wrong, though I wouldn't have wanted to make an entire career out of it.

I got out of my bed and prowled over to the window. I could hear traffic moving outside, and quite a lot of it. I peeled back a curtain and let the brightness of the day burn my eyes. It seemed my little cat nap had turned into something closer to the full eight hours.

It was time to move and the way I saw it there was only one place to go.

I got back in my car and counted my blessings. What a time to take my first decent lie-in since I could remember. Letting myself become a sitting duck - I couldn't believe that Jackson's men hadn't beaten my door down and hauled me back to my civic prison.

There was no question: this *had* to be a set up.

Starting up the engine I decided to give whoever might be following me a little excursion, free of charge. I'd learned enough about shaking a tail, God knows, and I pitied the poor soon-to-be-suffering-the-worst-case-of-car-sickness-in-his-or-her-life chump who had been assigned the task.

I went nowhere by the long route and then did the same again with inverted loops thrown in for good measure. By the time I pulled up outside the offices of my lunatic author, *I* was feeling car sick.

I parked up some distance from TMU's palace in the sky, in case my car might be spotted by one of Jackson's legion. Then I made my way to the Mighty One's tower.

A sense of bleak unreality stole over me.

Since those faraway days of *The Black Widow*, finding out it was TMU that I was working for - and had been all along – I had daydreamed about this place and about TMU. And because of the insanities of the present case, I had re-visited those offices in person and found half a story. *In person.*

But what's to say that *in person* meant anything. How could I enter a building, any building, that housed my author and my creator? TMU inhabited another world, and I inhabited this one, Chapeltown, the one that he had created for me. A place that existed only in the pages of *his* imagination.

TMU's offices were part of the fabric of his fictional creation. I could never meet TMU there – at best I could meet a representation of TMU, created by him the same way he had created me and all the others who lived here. So how could I meet the real TMU?

Maybe it was the drugs they had used on me, mixing nicely with the lack of food and a shortage of sleep that a single night of catching up could never entirely repair.

Whatever the secret, a doorway had opened.

Opened on the real TMU.

Or so it appeared...

I wasted no time, entering the inner sanctum; the engine room of TMU's working life. In a few moments I was fumbling at the drawer again, his secret drawer.

Out of nothing, with no prelude and no ceremony, I heard his voice. He was asking what I was doing there. And I was asking the same question. But there were no mouths moving on either side of the conversation.

We were two disembodied spirits talking to each other through the channel of pure mind. I was dreaming myself as the real me, drifting through the offices of creation. And that me was the eyes, the fingers, the facility to touch, to open a drawer, to lift out the most secret of all secrets.

But face to face with The Man Upstairs? No, not that. No faces.

I was a dream-embodied moveable figure in the shape of Frank Miller, otherwise how could I have penetrated this far into the enterprise? It was one thing to have peeked into a drawer and walked away with an intriguing question - but conversation?

The conviction settled over me: that I was spread out like a patient on a table, the mayor injecting me with travelling medicines, enabling me to take this journey of the mind and soul while he waited for the revelations to leak out of me.

Yet a dream could still take you only so far, even a drug-induced one, controlled by a monster; because at some point you woke up, had to, those were the rules of dreaming, any kind of dreaming. And then it was over, forgotten or dismissed until maybe the next time, and the next, like some recurring nightmare that took you nowhere. Who could ever lay store by treasures gained from mere dreaming?

And yet...

"What are you doing here, Frank?"

The voice of God. *My* God.

I looked around but the room appeared empty. I answered in the same fashion: "What are *you* doing here?"

"I live here. I work here. You were not invited, Frank. This is out of bounds. This is forbidden."

I placed my hand on the handle of the drawer.

"What are you doing? You can't go in there. My private papers – "

I was laughing. "Why don't you show yourself," I said. "Why not put this on an even footing? You see me, I see you. Don't let a bad hair day come between friends, what do you say?"

My hand tightened on the handle of the drawer.

"You know what I'm doing, don't you? I'm looking for clues. I'm a detective, in case you'd forgotten. This is what I do - try to make sense out of mystery. Order out of chaos. Those are the rules and that's the extent of them. I take a deck of cards, all shuffled out of order so that you can't make it out, and I start putting them back the right way. But you need a clue, at least one, and that sets you off. And soon enough you realise the nature of the game you're playing. You know whether it's hearts or spades, and you start making tricks; and if you're worth the name of *detective* you know enough to play the game better than the person who messed up the deck in the first place."

There was a long pause. I was looking at that unopened drawer, waiting to see what he had left before I went in.

"So what's different, Frank?"

I could hardly believe the question.

"*You're* are asking *me*? I'm not the one playing games. I've picked up some messed up decks before, but this one - I look at the cards I've been dealt and I see my own face stamped on the back of every one. And you're in there too, and that makes even less sense. We're not supposed to be in the deck, don't you know that? Especially not you."

"Things changed, Frank."

"What things? Tell me."

"You think you'd understand?"

"Try me. But how about first you show yourself, pull out a couple of chairs and bring in a bottle. If you want to play a part in your own detective story, why not do it in style?"

The voice went quiet. I waited. At last I said, "You still there?"

"I'm not going anywhere, Frank. This is my domain, remember. When I revealed the nature of existence to you, in *The Black Widow*, everything changed. Haven't you realised that yet?"

"Not everything changed. We still kept some house rules – some basic logic. I still had a deck of cards to shuffle around and we both knew when they were straight and our little world was back in order again. But now I'm in there, inside the deck, and you're in there – I can't know what game we're playing unless you at least give me some clues. I'm a reasonable guy, but you're asking too much."

"Too much? Have you no ambition? There's nothing new in an investigator having to do a little investigating of himself, Frank. And there's nothing new in an investigator doing a little investigating into the man who employs him. That's not what's new here."

"Now we're starting to get somewhere. So what's the new trick this time?"

"Wouldn't that spoil the game?"

"That good, is it? Is this going to be my most famous case - the one I'm to be remembered for above all the others?"

"I hope so, Frank. I hope it's the one *I'll* be remembered for, at least."

"Okay, let's not split hairs."

I eyed the drawer again with a sudden sense of despair. TMU sounded in control. I saw it slipping away. This was just another part of the game. I would open that drawer and find nothing but paper torn into confetti. Better to walk away from it, letting him believe that I was one step ahead of where he thought I was.

I pushed the idea away. Who was I fooling? I could never outwit him. The nature of the set-up would never allow for that degree of rebellion.

My hand tightened again on the handle of the drawer.

"Frank –"

I opened it.

Inside the drawer was a single envelope. I took it out.

I could hear him laughing.

"I don't know what happens now, Frank. I don't know what this will do to our…relationship."

I said, "I'm damned glad to hear that I'm not the only one working in the dark."

His laughter sounded hollow. "I mean to say, Frank. This really is *new territory*."

"Now you're stealing my phrases."

"No, I'm taking back the ones I lent to you in the first place."

There were a dozen or so sheets of paper inside the envelope, fastened by a single paper clip. I took the pages out and started reading.

All the baloney about the Mayor of Chapeltown was in there. It banged on about Nancy Tate dying, about the care agency – The Chapeltown Angels - Michelle Spar, Alice Coor, Rose Morton. Page Two kicked off with Trudi Tremain - and my time with Trudi was in there too. Reading it made it obscene and at the same time holy. Trudi took up the full page, with her mother a footnote.

Something struck me.

I thought about the stuff I'd read at the library, all the famous, celebrated cases of mine. All planned down to the last detail, meticulous, with nothing left to chance. Yet here it seemed that *everything* was left to chance. Random - no, more than that. *Like a first draft*. Like something that was finding its way as it went along. No design; no purpose. Cards drawn from different decks. Free fall. *Chaos*.

I carried on reading. The Town Hall, labyrinthine corridors, basements, drugs piped in, women wearing masks to protect them, sex and more sex, insatiable, tasteless, violent and pornographic.

Was I lying asleep in front of that giant screen, that altar to obscenity, or was this real, this scene in TMU's cosy private office, reading about it like it was some caper that might go this way and might go that. A series of whims, meaning nothing, altering nothing.

My curiosity was flattening out beneath a crushing weight. What revelation could lift all of this baggage out of the growing darkness spreading around me? What turnaround, or clue, or anything else could make me leave this room and this dream with a renewed sense of vigour?

Was this the end of the road, one way or another?

As I read on, I found myself hoping so.

I was reaching the end of it when his voice interrupted me.

"There's still time, Frank."

I didn't answer; I was bent on reading right to the end now. I was already at the bottom of the penultimate page, looking down Alice Coor's arse and into the blazing eyes of the Mayor of Chapeltown.

How poetic. How edifying.

Escape.

Sleep.

Entering the offices of TMU.

The secret drawer open; the papers in my hand.

Reading.

The past had caught up with the present. Maybe it wasn't so random after all. Maybe there was a plan. Of sorts. A poor one, but still a shape, a design. A rough draft. First thoughts and unmoulded ideas. Frank Miller had never lived in them before; Frank Miller only knew the finished thing, the final draft. He – I – had never lived in anything other than a *final draft,* and that, surely, was the way it should be.

As the thoughts bombarded me I heard his voice one last time.

"Now you see the conceit, Frank? Now you see the twist? You're going to like it, Frank. You're going to *love* it. Don't stop now – you're nearly there. Finish it, Frank."

I had reached the final paragraph. I stopped reading. "You never meant for me to see this, did you? This is a change of plan?"

But the voice was silent.

It remained silent.

I turned back to the page, half expecting to find it gone, vanished; expecting to find myself awake in my Town Hall basement suite, waiting for the next feature to start up on the screen.

But that's not what happened. I read on to the end.

I put the papers down on the desk and stood there, holding myself up against a filing cabinet to stop from falling over. I could barely breathe; everything was swimming inside me and around me. I wondered if my head had left my shoulders and was rolling down towards the door. I blacked out before I hit the floor.

I don't know how long I'd been out when a splinter of light nudged me, and I crawled back up to the desk where the scattered pages still lay. I picked them up, finding the last page and reading over it again, though I didn't need to. Those words would never be erased from my mind whatever happened.

This was a revelation to rank alone alongside my discovery of God. When I knew, that first time, that I was not a free and independent agent, but looked upon and cherished by a far greater authority. That I was nothing more than a made up character in a made up story. The work of another's imagination. A detective in a fantasy penned by a sick bastard with a fucked up sense of humour.

At least that revelation had come with a silver lining. Had come with the joy of immortality.

Now that joy was being blown out of the water. My darkest visions were being realised. My grotesque and far-fetched hunches proving true. The extraordinary nature of my being counting for nothing.

It was over.

TMU was planning the biggest murder of all.

The murder of Frank Miller.

NINETEEN: THE CASE OF THE BLACK WIDOW

My thirteenth case. The one where everything changed. The case of *The Black Widow*.

She was, without doubt, the finest femme fatale TMU ever created. No question about it. I miss her still. It's a tragedy that TMU couldn't find a way to bring her back into the series. Maybe...if he's listening...

But that's all academic now.

One day, out of the blue, she turned up at my door. Turned up with a tale to tell. There was a missing person and she wanted me to find him. The missing person was her husband, a man with the imaginative name of John Smith. She was worried about him. Distraught.

Heartbroken.

Then it turned out that John Smith wasn't missing at all. The *Black Widow* had got me on the case, but she knew it wasn't how it looked. She was what you might call, 'economical with the facts'. And then some. But I liked her, right from the start. Liked her a lot and she knew it.

And that was the problem.

As the case progressed it became clear that John Smith was up to both ears, dealing in every rotten scam in the book. She didn't mind him running out on the marriage, but she wanted some of the action. Wanted some of her investment back.

And that's where I came in.

Of course she wanted to blind me to the real situation, and, with the fine intuition of a true woman of the world, she figured out my soft spot on our very first meeting. She used her cunning and her charms to confuse me when the plot was really so straightforward that a third rate amateur could have cracked it while holding down two day jobs and a career in the Chapeltown police

I was hot on Smith's trail and by then I knew the extent of his dealings, though not the extent of hers. He was a police officer, medium ranking, with no great ambition in the job. His wife thought she was marrying a future D.I and began her marriage dreaming only of dinner-parties. But police balls were to remain the highlights on the calendar, and quickly things started to get rocky in the Smith house.

Then Johnny-boy has what looks, for all the world, like a mental breakdown. He visits the local witch-doctor who gives him some coloured sweets and some time off sick. Johnny-boy uses his time to get some *real* work done, setting up a few deals here and there and quietly rising through the ranks of the very underworld that he is supposedly dedicating his working life to defeating.

The sick note runs out and he goes back to the day job on limited duties. But pretty soon he's down again. Needing more time off. And you just can't get to the position of city godfather on the time off that the department is willing to give you. It can't be done.

His wife is a little smarter than the Chapeltown police and she knows something's going on that Johnny-boy isn't telling her about. There's talk of him being pensioned off, except that the doctors are not convinced. They don't smell a rat, but they do feel that this man still has plenty to offer, and they want to give him more time.

Time's the very thing that John Smith craves, but not in the sense that the police department mean. Not in the sense of getting himself back to work. He already has far more work than he can handle, because there isn't a racket in town that he hasn't got his fingers into.

The heat turns up and Johnnie-boy goes AWOL.

So Mrs. Smith comes into my office – the broken-down hut from which Frank Miller then operated, but still better than the no-office-at-all from which I currently operate. She comes in all full of worries and concerns about dear old poor and vulnerable Johnnie.

Enough to break a heart clean in two. Pure class. So me and the *Widow* go looking. Together. And along the way we discover that we have a few things in common. Like the joys of booking into country motels for a little mutual support of the physical kind, for instance, and all in the name of saving a marriage and solving the case of a vulnerable missing person.

The case is moving on steadily and we find ourselves out in the old country, the area surrounding Chapeltown and about two steps from getting to Smith himself. (In those innocent times I had believed in a country beyond Chapeltown. I think we all did. Turned out that it was another illusion. Another promise that would remain forever unfulfillied.)

We check into a place for the night. *The Third Eye*, if I remember correctly. A place where they didn't ask too many questions and didn't look at you too closely. It was during our stay there that things began to change. Little things at first. Suggestions that everything was not as it appeared to be.

I wanted to go easy on her; it seemed to me that she had enough pain and grief coming when she found out the full extent of what she was married to. But the questions were beginning to pile up.

Questions about the *Black Widow*.

Questions about the feelings stirring up inside me.

I was getting the sense that there were things lurking in the corners that I couldn't quite bring into focus. Feelings that I was not as in control of my destiny as I'd once believed myself to be. That I was being used. Manipulated. A puppet dancing to someone else's tune.

So I put the two sets of questions together and pretty much convinced myself that it was all down to the *Black Widow*. That she was the one pulling my strings. That she'd done such a job on me that I never even realised the extent of her power to control me.

It was the obvious conclusion. So I keep a closer eye and pretty soon I started making some interesting discoveries. Like, for instance, the fact that she'd been hot on Johnnie-boy's tail from the beginning. That she'd been using me like a pawn in a game of chess.

It all clicked into place. Naturally I kept it to myself, not letting on for a second that I'd got her sussed.

That same night, closing in on Johnny-boy, we returned to *The Third Eye,* which had become our base. She made it clear that she was feeling up for a little celebration. Now the *Black Widow* was not really a drinker, and so I had a good idea of the kind of rumpus she was in the mood to kick up. And let me tell you, she put old Frankie through his paces that night, and I'm still warm in the glow of the memories.

So anyway, we're lying together, shattered and still hungry, knowing the plan for the next day, when that feeling of being a puppet on a dirty piece of string swept through me like a fever. And even when the worst of it had passed it was still tugging like a bad tooth and I couldn't rest for it. So, late as it was, I got out of bed, fixed myself a drink, trying to bring something into focus that didn't want to come out into the light.

I'm standing in the doorway, sipping at my drink, watching her sleep. She's lying there like she hasn't a care in the world. She's going to find her husband, fake a glorious reunion, promise to take care of him and, between them, beat his illness.

So she's got it all set up, nice and simple. Frank as witness and Frank as insurance. Frank as the dumb flat-foot tying the two of them together; Frank thinking he's blessed because he earns the going rate for doing the lady a favour and not landing himself in the Chapeltown morgue.

My mind is running riot. I'm looking into that sleeping face and I can see the cracks appearing, like the beginnings of an earthquake. And inside those cracks I catch a glimpse – *of what*? - some inner, mysterious workings. Beyond even her comprehension.

Suggestions of a higher authority.

And I'm thinking all this, watching her sleeping, when suddenly her eyes open, and she looks up and sees me. She asks what's up, and I play it dumb.

Restless. Thirsty. Big day coming up.

But I can see that she doesn't believe any of it. So she plays her favourite trick and offers to take old Frank back to bed for some more play time. But she knows that's only going to keep the wolves at bay for so long. And so she changes the plot around.

She wants to make a deal.

Nail her no good husband and share the profits.

She thinks she's being rumbled.

She couldn't have been further from the truth.

But she doesn't know that and she tells me more than I need to know.

And now I see the extent of her deception. She wasn't called the *Black Widow* for nothing. She'd worked her way through a whole string of husbands and lovers and none of them had lived to tell the tale.

So now it's all making sense again. All that stuff about having my strings pulled - just proof that I was dealing with the greatest challenge of my career. She'd played me almost to perfection and I'd almost missed it. Only the gut instinct of Chapeltown's finest detective had saved me from becoming merely the latest victim of the infamous *Black Widow.*

It was my kind of tale and she was my kind of villain. Murder, double-cross and all its assorted relations was the life for a small town detective. And it was as much as my reading public wanted.

But now, though still unknown to me, TMU wanted to take it further. Wanted his small town dick to get all philosophical, turning a workaday plot on its head until nobody could be sure of anything.

Of course TMU did it a lot better than I'm making it sound. After all, he's the writer and I'm merely the gumshoe. He brought it on gradually. Started me off with the notion of the puppet-master. Gave me a solid suspect in the shape of his best ever female villain, then started to prepare the way for all kinds of weird twists, turns and finally those mind-bending revelations on the final strait.

Like I say, it was all very nicely done. Exquisitely done, in fact. On his day TMU could turn water into wine and a frog into a pond full of princesses and back again before nightfall. So he riffed for a while on the notion of me being sorely tempted by her offer. Let me wrestle with the temptation of partnering the *Widow*, killing off her husband and netting some profits, both of the flesh and of mere coinage.

145

I thought about her offer of a deal. I mean I gave it some real thought.

A bent Frank Miller.

The prospect amused me, and then, about one inch before morning's light came, it didn't amuse me at all.

I was thinking about myself like I was something separate from what I was using to do the thinking with. And when I got my head around that, she was already waking up to the big day; and instead of a straightforward wind-up, I was looking at an inner world filled with more drama and conflict than anything that I'd encountered on the streets of Chapeltown.

She recognised the tension, and did her best to ease me in that time-honoured way of hers. It worked, too, in the short term. She could see my distraction, but she thought it was all to do with me still weighing up the deal.

But Frank Miller taking the rats-road wasn't an option. It was not how I was made. And I was more than a little curious about that.

I mean, what exactly was keeping me on that side of the line?

And that's what finally caused the penny to drop the rest of the way down into the dirty black water at the bottom of the well.

TMU was still giving me the edge. He let me work out that a piece like her would never change for any man, not even for Frank Miller. That if I had weakened and joined forces with her, I would have ended up on the slab like all of her others did eventually, once she'd used them up.

So he had me fight off the temptation and collar the pair of them, but not without revealing glimpses of other forces at work. Not without letting me peer between the cracks and see the outline of another world and a higher power.

And at last I figured out that it wasn't her.

Once I started to question whether the *Black Widow* was the real puppet master, things went ballistic. Philosophy and violence, metaphysics, metafiction, mayhem and murder mixing together like old pals at a barn dance for the damned. And he'd prepared it like a pro, and in the end he pulled it off and kept his readers into the bargain.

The readers loved that book and the world went Miller crazy. They couldn't get enough. But the damndest thing was this: that the moment I realised that there was a *Man Upstairs*, I started to question him. I wanted to know what the hell he was playing at. If *he* had given me the case of John Smith and his *Black Widow* wife, why was he ruining the tale by throwing in all that hocus-pocus about Frank Miller becoming aware that somebody up there was pulling his strings?

As far as I was concerned, Frank Miller wasn't the kind of detective to get hung up on what you might call a…existential crisis. It just didn't ring the right kind of bell. Tracking down John Smith and dealing with his sting-in-the-tail wife – oh, that was Frank territory. That was *classic* Frank territory. The hotels, the offer of a deal – I had no complaints with any of that stuff.

But *The Man Upstairs* baloney was like something a cheap editor had tacked on as a joke, and not a particularly funny one.

Only later did it dawn on me that TMU did what he did because he had run into a dead end. He brought on an *existential awakening*, for God's sake!, to distract the readers from the muddle of a plot that he didn't

147

know how to resolve. He chose to make his greatest creation, Frank Miller himself, aware of the facts of his true existence simply because he had run out of steam.

A way out.

A cop out.

Sleight of hand - and somehow he'd pulled it off.

Got away with it.

And I couldn't help but admire him.

And once I started to admire him, it grew out of all proportion. It grew to the extent of believing that maybe I had been wrong all the way. That TMU knew what he was doing after all. Knew exactly what he was doing and in every sense and from the very beginning.

That it was all down to faith.

That I was in safe hands.

That I had nothing to fear...

On the outer rim of Chapeltown's remote county boundary, where the land rises up into the hills, we found John Smith, as I never for a moment doubted that we would. As the tale grew to its climax and conclusion, I knew that nothing had been in doubt from the start. It had all been written. Frank was going to collar the pair of them.

And that's how it played out.

Picture this:

She's walking to the police van, stops, asks what could keep a man from nailing a villain, winning the girl and making so much money that he could leave Chapeltown for good. And suddenly everything stops. The silence is deep enough to drown a world in. It's like I'm standing back, waiting to hear my own reply.

Old Frankie poised in the moment, not wanting to ruin a perfectly good ending telling her that none of them could ever leave Chapeltown because Chapeltown was where the world began and ended. And Old Frankie too old-school to let on that 'winning the girl' wasn't all it was cracked up to be when she was likely to poison a man one day and for good measure eat him the next.

And so I watched myself play Frank Miller; watched myself settling for the line that had been prepared for me. Possibly the most celebrated line in the entire series. The line that coined the immortal phrase and gave the author a name that would ring eternal.

With a tired, cynical glimmer of a light somewhere in the back of my eye, I placed my mouth right next to the *Black Widow's* ear and whispered, "What would keep me from all that? Let me tell you: *The Man Upstairs, baby.*"

They led her away with a look on her face worth all the gold ever mined, in this town or any other. But I knew that the gold was no longer Frankie's.

The tale ended in trademark style, Frank Miller in the arms of some bimbo unrelated to the case. A piece of warmth who knew nothing of a mythical land beyond Chapeltown, but a lot about how to complement a fine whisky through a long night.

On the page I must have looked the happiest man alive. But hiding between the lines was a new kind of desperado.

The Black Widow was the thirteenth in the series and the most loved, according to the sales charts. Those faithful readers who had come to love Frank Miller, after stroking their brows, shaking their heads, reserving their judgements – they all seemed to make their minds up at the same delay-setting, and so a star was born.

They were preaching my name out in the streets, and in the bars and cafés. Frank Miller was everywhere: tee-shirts, posters, mugs and towels. And with the hysteria came the re-publication of all the other books, in fancy new editions. The whole canon back on the shelves and selling faster than it ever did the first time around.

Not that I had seen any of that the first time around.

Back then I was content to solve cases, and to get on and do what I was created to do. For precisely one dozen cases that was enough for me. And then TMU raised his quill for the thirteenth time and blessed me with the knowledge, extending my horizons beyond the covers of the books that held my sordid tales of cheap heroism in a cardboard town.

I had been some half-life in a literary coffin, re-animating whenever he thought fit to open the lid and let in a little light. And when he was done with me, I would be banished from the kingdom, back into my temporary tomb until the next time.

I got to like the notion of my readers bringing me back to life every time they held a copy of a Miller mystery. Cynicism can be a heavier burden than naivety, and I wear that tee-shirt on my free evenings and public holidays.

Of course the questions kept coming. Why couldn't TMU have taken me to one side when I was in-between cases? A quiet word in my ear? Why did he have to do it, not only on the page, in public, but in the heat of my toughest challenge?

I have my theories, of course. That he wasn't so sure that the case had the legs. The critics were getting clever and the public restless, expecting something more than the traditional formula.

Yet I don't believe that it all came down to plotting difficulties. I happen to think that there was more to it. That TMU was going through a crisis of his own.

So okay, he wasn't sure where the case was going and needed to do something fast and radical. Fair enough. *Perhaps.* But on top of that he was drinking more than Frank Miller himself while penning all of that baloney. Some picture: TMU sitting in that glass and steel office of his, wondering where Frank was going next, what Frank was going to say next, the pair of us drinking each other under the table and running out of life.

I don't know the drafts that went into it, I only have what you out there have: the evidence of what finally made it on to the published pages.

A private detective hot on the trail of corruption and blackmail, tempted first by the lust of a bad woman and then by the greed that was consuming everybody else around him.

TMU trying to thicken up my character; waking me from my dogmatic slumbers; waking himself up, and maybe even his readers.

And while Frank was blowing his brains out in the arms of that poisonous bitch, TMU pulled the stroke on him and threw the cards in that messed-up deck to the mercy of the winds that were blowing through the badlands of Chapeltown.

Poor Frank sitting up on the bed, the *Widow* still warm from the rumpus they'd been making, getting cold quickly around the eyes and looking at him in a way he didn't recognise.

"*You know, don't you?*"

151

The certainty fading in an instant, leaving nothing but cross-purpose and confusion. The *Widow* thinking she was looking through all that deception and already wondering how to do the big dirty on Frank and when and where.

And all the time Frank, seeing but not seeing, his mind circling an alien land, wondering how he could have lived his entire life as a fictional detective and never seen the signs.

Frank Miller and the Existential Crisis.

But maybe just a beginner's crisis.

A warm up exercise to get old Frankie ready for the real torture chamber of the soul that was to come later with The Mayor of Chapeltown and his council from hell.

As the great detective sat bolt upright on that bed next to the *Widow*, entering the last section of the book, he guessed that no-one before had ever had to bear the realisation that he was nothing but a character in the pages of fiction. But what did that matter? What did he care about prizes for originality?

Fiction! It burned in the blood.

Frank Miller - a mere creation of some alcoholic writer!

How did it go after that?

Anger first..?

Then the self-pity..?

It went like this:

Frank Miller looking away from the *Widow*, staring out of the window at nothing at all. She was getting edgy. Distracted, was old Frank, but not insensible to her movements. She was close to him, and he had to keep at least one eye on the game. She wanted to know what was wrong and he had to tell her something.

His mind was racing like it was one minute to closing time. He couldn't hold her off. Had to say something, and say it fast.

She touched him, a hand on his arm. This was his cue, his last chance to save the hour.

And then it occurred.

To turn back to her, look her in the eye, perhaps even take her hand and say, Look, honey, I'm not what you think I am. My name really is Frank Miller, but I'm not here and neither are you. I'm a fictional hero, living in a book, a series of books. I'm what you would call, technically, a *series-character*. And you are in one of my books. You are a character in one of *my* stories – that's you, your son-of-a-bitch of a husband, and every other low-life in this literary hard-on.

The thought of saying all that cracked me up. I couldn't hold it. It all came out, but not in words.

Laughter, gallons of it, filled the room, the sky; it went out like a cloud and it covered Chapeltown to the extent of its imprecise boundaries that nobody could ever get an angle on and likely never will.

So eventually the laughing stopped. She looked at me like she no longer thought I'd cracked the case, but more likely cracked my head. And I thought that insanity need not ruin a perfectly good opportunity in life, and so I took the perks, and she didn't seem any less satisfied with the fictional Frank than she had been a little earlier in the arms of the so-called real one.

It didn't make any difference at all.

Was actually quite liberating, the more I thought about it.

And so for the rest of that evening I was either laughing or indulging myself around the considerable delights of the company I was keeping.

And I think that all my activity that night weakened her. And by the end of it maybe some of her resolve was already slipping. Maybe she was falling in love with old Frankie.

You see how TMU did that?

He turned it all around in that revelation. Not only did he give his readers something off the planet to think about, distracting them while he got me out of the muddle he'd created. But at the same time he used all of my new found energy to satiate her and make it all the more credible that she might become distracted.

Sleight of hand – that's all there's ever been, really. And this time TMU really laid it on thick. He distracted everybody so that by the end of it all, the last thing on the reader's mind was some trivial inconsistency or the slight overstretching of credibility.

All through the story there had been things not adding up. All through there was a tickle of disbelief. You want to make people forget the little tickles, and itches, and minor irritations bugging them – just belt them in the face and see all those problems disappear in a haze of pain.

And that's what he did. Call it laziness, call it desperation. He hit the readers so hard in that last quarter that it was all they would see and all they would care to remember. TMU belted them in the face and they loved him for it like they'd never loved him before.

Of course, in that book, I was reeling a little myself. But things settled down as the fourteenth book in the series came and went. I was finding new fun, new ways to rise to the stranger challenges that TMU was giving me. New beginnings and new adventures yet still a healthy helping of the old indulgences that were always there to anchor things down, keep the thing rooted and keep both Frank and his public satisfied.

Now I had God in my life, a creator whom I knew about. I had a personal identity and a hand in the shaping of it, or so I believed.

And then that faith – and later that doubting of faith - too became one of my themes.

For a while it was like TMU couldn't lose. This new angle enriched everything. Any sticking points, any weakness in a plot line, any problem that couldn't be resolved using the old methods – it all seemed grist to the mill. He could throw any old crap at the page and it dripped out a fountain of gold at the end. The books were selling off the scale and nobody was prepared to set any limits. You picked up a Frank Miller mystery and anything might happen, and usually did. And that kind of expectation…I tell you, if you need telling: we couldn't lose and we knew it.

What times they were.

What times.

His form went through the roof. He was shining with it. He'd always had some degree of talent, but he'd spent so long trying to drown it that too many had written him off.

But he hadn't drowned it. Liquid of any kind was the wrong method of metaphor entirely, unless you're talking about liquid nitrogen. He was on fire. He was blazing. The ideas were exploding out of him night and day and I felt more alive than I ever did in the days before I knew what my nature really was. I was more real than real. I was out of my shell, truly alive, a *real boy*.

In one scene, in the eighteenth book, I was dancing around singing the song from *Pinocchio,* about having no strings to hold me down. I was drunk, but the

155

man holding my puppet levers was as sober as the judge that Chapeltown apparently needed in the nineteenth book, the last but one before this present farce.

The cracks were beginning to show.

The twentieth saw the cracks widening and the fire dying down. Sales were still up on past glories but the critics went for blood, prophesying that unless the author came up with something extraordinary, the series was dead.

One reviewer had also read the story of the wooden boy, and he didn't intend wasting the experience:

A potted history of the wooden detective of Chapeltown:

One through twelve and he doesn't even know he's made of wood. Thirteen smacks creation across the ear until its head spins, and the hero finds out the world isn't what it seems and that his creator makes Gepeto seem like the sanest geek in fairy-tale creation. Then Frank hits his stride as the strings are cut, finds his way in this new world – the same old Chapeltown, but as changed as a bed when the corpse lying next to you turns into the woman of your dreams and back again before morning.

Your wooden boy, Gepeto, has become real!

But has run out of stories.

Let's hope and pray that Frank Miller never comes of age.

He must die, here, aged Book Twenty. We must not be forced to endure his Twenty-First!

Some wit, eh?

I thought again of the *Widow* and every other character in the canon: The good, the bad, the downright infectious; killers, blackmailers, aspiring saviours; the saints turned sour and the legions of damned redeemed - and it struck me that I loved every last one of them.

But the road was ending. TMU was listening to his critics again, just like he did after book twelve. But you can't play the same trick twice. I could picture the advertising: *Twenty one! Frank Miller comes of age!*

I should have been out celebrating a glorious denouement with a fresh bimbo lined up for the epilogue.

Some twenty-first this was shaping up to be.

What could I do? I'll tell you. I went on the biggest nostalgia trip of all, back over all my cases from the first day sitting in my hole-for-an-office, watching the obligatory blonde come to the glass and bring me a tale about love and blackmail. A tale that quickly and inevitably turned to murder, then double murder.

We always started out with a mystery, and as Frank got enmeshed, started sticking his neck out, we hammed up the suspense. Sometimes it took a while, but Frank always got there in the end, nailed the villain and offered his wit-riddled, homespun philosophy all packaged up with threads from a silver tongue, and polished off with a killer line. Then the final obligation, taking a bottle to bed to make up a threesome - and that's how they all ended.

No Frank Miller tale of mystery and suspense complete without a bottle and a girl and both getting full honours right on that final page.

All the way through twelve books.

Next to nothing ever changing.

157

It's what the reading public wanted when it picked up a Miller Mystery. Re-assurance. Solid ground. Frank gets the bad guy, does what he does, order restored and the world goes on turning. Frank Miller, a guy you can depend on. Dependable old Frank, in twelve paperbacks, all in the same cheap jackets housing sixty thousand words or as near as makes any difference.

Then the critics get tetchy and TMU starts messing. Starts tipping back the bottle and then tipping it back some more. Shaking hands shaking things up. Taking hold of the town he'd created and *shaking it*.

The *Black Widow* case - the first signs of TMU's growing sickness. Literary experimentation - that's what he called it. All the time I was thinking that I was going crazy. A case not adding up, cards falling and never making hands. It could have been the end of TMU. Should have been - according to the *experts*.

And they all got it wrong.

Frank was never bigger.

And then they all looked back, the retrospective angle, and saw the trick and suddenly it's all yes, of course, it couldn't fail. It was what the world was waiting for and every reader worth their salt should have seen it.

At first those hacks think it's one formula replacing another. But little by little they have to concede that TMU really is a case on his own. He doesn't play it straight, he changes it every time. Because now that Frank knows – now that he has blessed him with consciousness – TMU starts letting go of the reins, getting out of the way and letting Frank tell his own stories.

Now you start reading a Miller mystery and you can't guess the end by page three.

Except that you can still guess the very end because TMU understands style, too. And after all of that literary experimentation, he knows enough to realise that any reader going through all of that needs a little home comfort at the end. And so it's off to bed with the whisky bottle and the broad just like old times.

Nobody's complaining.

And in twenty mysteries there hasn't been a single occasion when Frank hasn't left the reader's company in that fashion.

Yet I can't see it happening this time.

Because the critics have been sharpening knives again and the book sellers getting nervy and that's all it takes to make the great TMU decide to make this, the 21st Frank Miller mystery, the last in the series.

What about responsibility? A creator's responsibility towards his creation?

…Or is the onus on the creation itself?

On me?

Could I still save the day?

The belief in myself – the belief that I could turn all of this around and save the day - flared up within me and then just as quickly flickered out.

I turned around and faced it. The future. My future. What kind of death might a fictional death be? Not so much the detail, the does he take up with a spiked bottle or else wind up with more holes in him than the wrong kind of Chapeltown cheese. No, what I was wondering was: does the fictional death leave out the unpleasantries and concentrate on the heroic?

Or is it even crueller?

I could feel another existential crisis – or maybe another angle on an already existing one – coming through. I was thinking: realisation that one is fictional is still, after all, a realisation of existence. The death is

159

still real. The promise of an imagined eternity snatched away. Does it – can it – get any worse than that?

So now I can die. I mean *really* die. The stakes have been raised and they don't get any higher. I know what's coming – but what can I do about it? Are the cards already marked?

Already dealt?

Despite Gepeto making me into a real boy, cutting my strings and setting me free - ultimately, in spite of everything, I have as much power to change my destiny as I had when I was going along through twelve good books and oblivious to all of this *reality.*

Precisely none.

The ultimate cruelty, as far as I can make out, is making your creation aware of its existence and then letting it know, by accident or design, that its days are numbered. He was committing the gravest sin of the first-person narrative and killing off the voice telling the tale.

Yet no jury would convict him.

Not in these postmodern fucked up times.

The clock was ticking on old Frankie.

I tried to figure out a plan.

It was too easy to give it up, to get all philosophical as an excuse against doing anything. That's the trouble with an existential crisis, in my experience. They sap your strength and then they take away your will to live. You come around to the idea of destiny: that everything's inevitable, and then you have no fight left inside you.

Since discovering the truth in Book Thirteen, I'd clung to the belief that a simple fact would save me. That whatever the danger, however pungent the pickle, the technical matter remained that all the Miller stories were related in the first person.

As long as I was telling the tale I was indestructible.

You can't kill off the voice telling the tale.

That's the rule.

Or is it?

Wasn't I forgetting about the very thing that had first given me life: *experimentation.*

And now, in my midnight hour, I got my memory back and recognised the smell rising up from the graveyard:

Literary experimentation could prove fatal and had done on countless occasions.

There were no rules anymore.

TMU was free to do anything he damned well chose to do.

Or was I letting it all get a little out of hand? Was it all far more humdrum? Some harmless fun that went too far because of a little thing called female malice?

My thoughts scuttled over the facts of the case. The scenes and conversations that had already formed the first half of the tale: Trudi's call. Michelle Spar's spite at the mention of Trudi's name. Signing Trudi's death warrant down by Chapeltown's river of sludge – and then signing it again in Trudi's bed.

Were we followed from the beginning? Was I the fall guy from the beginning? Was the mayor aware of it all from the beginning? Had he conspired against me *from the beginning...?*

I had visited TMU's citadel and found him out. Exposed him and his great secret.

That Frank Miller was going to die.

That the turnaround twist in this particular tale was to be the death of the hero and the end of the series.

161

Twenty-one was Frank's number after all.

My eyes opened on the truth of it.

The tired old cliché had to come of age.

It was all down to me.

I had to show TMU that there was life left in Frank Miller. Show him that pandering to critics and publishers was the road to destruction. I had to show my fallen author a way to resolve his tale in the traditional style, but with a twist so devastating it would satisfy every reader, critic, professor and living-breathing fiction-loving soul in the living-breathing world. I had to show TMU how to save his hero in the best book of the series.

I was waking from a dream of being alive to find the hangman waiting. The truth written in rainbow lights on a billboard that stretched across the Chapeltown sky:

Frank Miller has to change.

Marge was right.

It was the one thing that could save me.

TWENTY: OUT OF THE CORNER OF THE EYE

Perhaps, after all, it was no good thinking back over celebrated solutions, all documented and leather-bound in the Chapeltown library. Perhaps I could plunder those pages until the kingdom came and the kingdom went, but it would do no good because the rules had changed.

And then again, perhaps Jackson was full of shit.

I sat amongst TMU's scattered pages and wrestled with the notion that, even though the rules had changed, there were guiding principles operating underneath, at a deeper level. That some rock-bottom deal ran deeper than words on the page, and that a fiercer truth could still be extracted and returned to its rightful place in the treasury.

Not gold waiting to be mined so much as magic waiting to be pulled out by the roots.

This was a battle of wits. Jackson wanted me to submit to his will, to shrink until I was small enough for him to crush between his fat fingers. He had let me back out into the world on a length of rope.

I thought about *The Black Widow*, and one thought led to another until I had a cast of hundreds running around the inside of my head. I tried to pin Jackson down, the character I had not seen building through the mysteries.

Why hadn't I seen him?

Because I had looked too hard at *me*.

It was easy blaming TMU for giving me a shit load of self-consciousness. The truth was that at heart Frank Miller was a self-centred son of an egomaniac. Selfish and small-minded, father and son. Yet if I was to survive beyond the pages of the present nightmare, I couldn't spend the rest of my existence merely *blaming* that egomaniac.

I had to act.

Fast.

I tried to get an angle on the Jackson character in the previous books, but I could still hardly see him at all. I needed to be out of here, down at the Chapeltown library, finding something about him that could alter the balance.

These drafts were no good to me. I didn't need the working out, I needed the finished articles.

Or did I?

The mayor had slipped in the back door. Not planned in draft and re-draft, but stealing in against the tide of TMU's best intentions.

The more I tried to focus on the books, the less I could see.

Some things are best glimpsed out of the corner of an eye.

So I tried an old trick: tried thinking about something else.

But I wasn't so easily fooled. Not by my own games. I was kidding myself that I was only using the corner of my eye when all the time I was still looking at the problem head on.

And then it happened.

Just like that.

Marge came in and saved me.

For no reason I could think of, I was thinking about blue pyjamas. Wishing I was lying in a different bed in a different room and easing her out of those blue Frank-teasers.

First off I was seeing Marge out of the corner of my eye.

Then I was looking at her centre screen.

164

And that's when I saw something glinting in the corner; and that light blinked on in my head full beam and I saw, at last, the first stirrings of the future Mayor of Chapeltown.

I saw it all in gothic style, a split-second inner-lightning flash, and then I turned that inner-eye in the direction of the Great Fat One and watched it become lost in the darkness again. Yet my memory retained the image; wouldn't let it go. I put my face into my hands to keep what I already had, and switched my head on full blast.

All the time that I had spent travelling around Chapeltown with the *Widow*, those elections had been bubbling away. As we prepared to head out for the country, we passed the Town Hall, passed the man on the corner, a shadow of a man, right outside the offices, standing on a soapbox, telling the good people of Chapeltown why they should vote for him.

It had all been so much background; texture and nothing more. But no question, it was him; maybe a few pounds lighter, and possibly a tad less ugly – *but it was him.*

What was he saying? Were the words written into the book? Was he just an image, fleshing out the scene, giving depth to what was happening in the foreground? Even so, he had to be saying something that resonated against the words and movements of the *Widow* and me. His words must have been down on the page, or else the character would have been meaningless.

I needed some peripheral perspective. So I concentrated on the blue pyjamas, and what lay beneath them. It wasn't difficult and it comes with practice.

And while I was focusing on Marge, the corner of my mind's eye was twitching; dig, dig, digging at the soil that covered ancient knowledge; and then it came, with a breathless rush.

The mayor was telling the people of Chapeltown that things were not as they seemed; that corruption didn't always come in the form of a man holding a violin case, or with a cigarette hanging out the corner of a crooked mouth; that the worst of men as often as not came dressed as the best of men, and the women of Chapeltown deserved better.

I had heard those words at some level and taken them as mere symbols: that obliquely he was telling, not the people of Chapeltown, but the readers of the Frank Miller mysteries exactly what was going on with the main players in the story.

In my ego-riddled head he was talking about me.

About me fixing the villain.

About me saving the town from yet another epidemic of evil.

Such was the egomania that I bore.

Son of my father.

Puppet of TMU.

Now I could see that there had been a good deal more at work. TMU was cleverer than I had given him credit. There were more levels than I could have uncovered in fifty mysteries, whatever the size of my PI's magnifying glass.

And there he was in the next book, a bit-player once again, but with a campaign trail hotting up nicely. With more oblique comments about Frank Miller passed off as some weird humour, manoeuvring himself into position with subtlety and cunning until the pay-off finally came, the mask ripped off: behold, the true saviour of Chapeltown.

Or its destroyer.

That's not how I'd read the signs back then, if I'd bothered to read them at all – which clearly I hadn't. I had been too comfortable. Too content to take the easy road and the perks that were on offer.

I was moving through the books now, using those blue pyjamas shamelessly. They were coming down and with them the blocks I had erected against self-knowledge. In my head I was up to the hilt in Marge, all the time stripping at the layers built up, book by book, case by case – the creation of the Mayor of Chapeltown.

His speeches, his manipulations, his rise to power - all consummately measured and planned. A sub-plot growing out of nothing. The merest fragment. And it had blossomed like a black seed into the present tale.

I was appalled at the beauty of the construction. For now I could see it full on. I ran the ending of my last book through my head: Walking through the Chapeltown streets like the legendary gunfighter, emerging from the smoke, heading into the arms of the whisky-bearing girl, celebrations going on all around me – and I had been too proud, too pre-occupied, to notice.

They were not celebrating the slaying of another villain, or the restoration of order in the town. They were popping corks because the mayoral elections had come and gone and one fat man was standing back on the podium making the kind of promises that only professional liars and mass-murderers would ever attempt.

It had all seemed like chords supporting a melody; the backdrop against which my walk of victory would appear all the more amazing.

Into the arms of the waiting girl, bottle in her hand, Frank on her arm. The traditional ending to every Frank Miller mystery.

But this time with a fat man firing the cork in the background.

In the last book the devil was buying his ticket into the world and riding through the rolls of fat accumulating around the belly of the mayor.

I didn't see it, any of it. But I was seeing it now – and what was it telling me?

That my faith was ebbing? Or that I was giving TMU too much credit? Was he capable of orchestrating such grandiose schemes? Wasn't he at heart just a hack who had made it lucky?

Or was his art subtler than he was ever given credit for? Did he specialise in disguising it? Hiding his true light under a bushel?

No, he couldn't create on that level, on that scale. He hadn't the depth, the subtlety. He could fashion a character, give him some blood and a few bones; put him in a situation and stand back and see what happened next. And something always did, to his credit. But he could not, any day of the week, plan all that was to come and work it up with such restraint over years and hundreds and thousands of pages.

Not TMU.

He dug out the idea of giving me self-knowledge – *real* self-knowledge - from the crazy notion that he could duck out of some of the work, leaving it to his leading man to come up with the lines; observing the fireworks from a safe distance – and out of sheer idleness, letting that character – me – and now even an elected mayor! - write the whole damned thing for him and to hell with the consequences.

I call that, not genius, but dereliction of duty.

Of course the critics came to find it all commendable, at least for a time; conspiring to redefine lazy habits as experimentalism of the highest order.

But critics never stay friends with you for long.

I walked across TMU's office, over to the window, and looked down from that great height over the town that he had created, piece by piece, book by book. Some parts unfinished, still in development. In the far distance I could make out the Honeywall Flats. What would Marge be doing? Or did her consciousness lie dormant when she was not on the page?

My head had loosened, rolled off my shoulders, but I was no longer concerned. The pain of all that thinking was worse than any outcomes at the over-sized hands of the mayor - or the writing hand of TMU.

So I decided, there and then, as I gazed over toward the Flats, to hand Marge the reins. To grant her permission to do as she pleased and make what she could out of the poor goods - if she still wanted them.

My creator had been a lazy god, and illness and professional critics had done the rest. With cards like that you learn fast to become a philosopher, though ultimately it can do you no good at all.

And so the moment came, the light flooding mind, body and spirit until I was *swimming* in it. Not surprising, then, in the presence of all that light that at last I saw what had for so long eluded me. That there was some good left inside TMU.

Why? There was good inside him because he had created Marge.

He had created her for a reason.

An idea was touching at the inside of my skull but it wouldn't come into focus. I thought again about the shadowy figure of the man who would one day put

169

on the robes of civic responsibility and declare himself the Mayor of Chapeltown.

The idea was knocking. What was needed was a scene. A single scene that would turn everything upside down.

A scene outside the Town Hall that would tear up what had started there during the case of *The Black Widow*...

TWENTY ONE: THE SICKNESS AND THE CURE

I drove past the Honeywall Flats certain that I wasn't being followed. Even so I didn't risk it. No way was I going to take chances with the life of the one person in Chapeltown who could save me. Who maybe had already saved me. The one person who I now held *precious.*

I drove on, not stopping until I was pulling up outside my hole.

I spent some time under the shower thinking. The water was cold enough to drive even the thoughts of blue pyjamas out of my head, leaving me with space enough to contain the fat reality of Thomas Jackson, and how I might confront him and lay him to rest.

It took fifteen minutes of brutal pain, but it was worth every second.

It was ingenious. It was insane. It was the truth.

I dried off and put on the uniform of the fictional detective once more. I knew the cards in the deck, all of them. Had always known, at some level at least, that shuffling them into the winning hand, Frank Miller style, was the torturous road to the public heart.

The road to salvation.

I laid them out straight.

The Mayor of Chapeltown, our own fat Mr. Thomas Jackson, had been an aberration growing in TMU's mind since the case of the *Black Widow*. Not so much an idea as a subliminal seed. And that seed grew, out of dark roots, into something twisted and bitter. I had discovered the true meaning of self-consciousness in that book, and the idea had leaked out and into the background figure on the steps outside the offices of the mighty.

Or at least the corporate mighty.

And so a plan grew to take over the series, highjack the Miller mysteries, killing-off Frank Miller himself.

TMU hadn't been well. And the mayor knew it. And he knew how to twist illness, idleness and literary conceit around his fat fingers.

If TMU had been in his right mind, none of this would have come about. You didn't throw in the towel on a series that was turning you into the undisputed champ. Sanity would, at some point, have prevailed. It had to, by every law that could make any universe tick.

But it *had* come about, and we were stuck with it. And TMU needed help. Practical help of the Frank Miller kind. Being philosophical would see me squashed like a fly beneath the wobbling gut of our great mayor.

The series was hanging by a thread. And with it TMU's beautiful career. The cards tumbling into a series of tricks. I could read them like the books of my life. In every one, a moment of crisis, though never before explicit; the battleground never so evidently the terrain of the author's troubled mind.

Enough experimentation? Enough game playing by a writer failing to realise how high the stakes had been raised? He lets his characters do all the work and where does it leave him?

A showdown between the extremes of his personality; a battle for sanity and soul.

So much light because that was my role. So much darkness because that was his, Thomas Jackson, mayor of this town.

If my cynicism helped bring on TMU's illness, I'd made up for it a thousand times already, keeping him this side of the asylum gates. *Keeping him in print.*

172

There was no way around Jackson's movie; TMU had his heart set on it. All the scenes that made no sense; all of those incoherent episodes - edited they would hang together as though a magic-wand had been waved across the cutting-room floor, making a tapestry from plastic and sawdust.

It was the oldest story of them all. Dark against light. Sickness against cure.

The mayor against Frank Miller.

Jackson figures he has all the answers along with the best lines, hiring me as the fall guy. He's the sickness inside of TMU.

And I'm the cure.

I had to hold onto that. Convince TMU. Convince a certifiable genius turned lunatic that the hero wins and wisdom prevails. Show him an ending that would bust his brains out. An ending where the light and only the light claims the prize. Become the Frank that TMU had in mind when he started this, the twenty-first in the series. The Frank Miller that TMU had glimpsed and then lost sight of. The new Frank. The Frank who through Marge could ditch the baggage once and for all and *change*.

"That's right, you mad bastard. Your son – your dearest Frankie, coming of age, ready or not."

And I had one scene to accomplish everything. One scene that I still couldn't see yet had to find.

The turnaround.

The twist.

I knew it had to take place outside the Town Hall and I knew that I needed as many people watching as I could get. Maybe even the whole of Chapeltown.

And that's all I knew.

173

I pulled up outside my hole expecting a welcoming committee. There wasn't even the notion of life itself. Neither daylight nor darkness. No clue as to what mood The Man Upstairs had assumed to greet the hour.

I felt alone in a universe that had been abandoned.

Maybe he had moved on to create somewhere else and forgotten that I had been left behind in a place once known as Chapeltown.

TWENTY TWO: FRANK'S BIG SOLILOQUY

I made some coffee and found that my comfortable chair was finally living up to the name.

Was somebody up there feeling a little guilty? I doubted it.

I waited for the phone to ring. Did a tour of the available explanations for the absurdities under which I was living. Even gave TMU the benefit of some of my thinking, delivering my big soliloquy, same as I've done in twenty other voyages through the insane world of The Man Upstairs.

"That escape's fooling nobody, pal. A cheap twist that not even you could pull off. A warning, perhaps? From Jackson and his band of angels bent on hijacking the series? College professors re-affirming their cheap moral laws from ivory towers and out of general disdain for the reading public?

"So you have them follow me, see that I'm safely home, minding my own business mostly, if still a touch curious. And now you're not so sure which way to go with this loony tune, so you buy a little time and space, treading a little water – am I right?

"Maybe there is a way to crack this case after all. A way to keep old Frank alive to fight another day - what do you say? Do I go out of here and wake Chapeltown out of its slumbers, or does that phone ring and we wait and see?"

I ended my big soliloquy and listened to the silence. When I couldn't stand the sound of my breathing, I continued bending the invisible ear, throwing down the gauntlet.

"The phone has another sixty seconds and then Frank goes to market."

The phone was ringing. I answered it.

A voice spoke softly. "What do you mean by that, Frank?"

The voice sounded familiar.

I said, "Who is this?"

"Don't play games with me, Frank, you're really in no position. *What do you mean by that?"*

"Mean by what, exactly?"

"Frank goes to market?"

I was trying to say something when I heard the click at the other end.

I sat back in my chair. "Okay," I said, though the line was broken. "I can take a joke as well as any man who *never* lived. But, well, I'm what you might call 'touchy' at the moment. My fuse has shortened; I can't for the life of me think why that should be. So it's another thirty seconds and then all hell breaks loose."

The door burst open.

Four men with guns came in without an invitation from me. All of the guns were pointing straight into my face. The men stood around me in a semi-circle but didn't say anything. I could hear shoes creaking beyond the doorway and I looked to see a figure coming through.

I recognised him straight away, even though the last time I saw his face it was framed between Alice Coor's buttocks.

"Oh, what an honour," I said. "If I'd known you did house calls, I could have saved myself some time and grief."

Thomas Jackson, the Elected Mayor of Chapeltown was, by any known measurement, a large man, with a neck so fat his chain of office must have been welded at a boatyard. And I wanted to tell him that; share my pithy observation and get some rapport moving in the room.

But he had other ways of getting a conversation started. He pulled back one of his meaty paws and swiped it across my chops. I felt my tongue taking an involuntary tooth count. I was fairly sure that nothing was missing, but a pulse pounded at the side of my jaw all the same.

Maybe he was telepathic. Maybe that swipe was just for thinking about telling him that he had more fat around the gills than any pig on an average day at the fair. And maybe he heard *that* thought, too. Because a moment later there was a pulse pounding away at the other side of my face, and the Mayor of Chapeltown was holding onto his fist like he'd damaged it against some hard nut's jawbone.

I held my face and said, "Afternoon to you, too."

That got him laughing, but it was hard to tell if it was a good sign. I said, "TMU send you, did he? Teach me a lesson for thinking aloud? Or thinking at all?"

He looked blank. "TMU?"

"Doesn't matter," I said. "Let it go."

But he didn't want to let it go. "Who's TMU - your boss?"

"You could say that."

A glint came into the mayor's eyes. "Lives at the top of the world, by any chance?"

"So you followed me?"

"Wanted to make sure you were safe, Frank. We care about you."

"How touching."

If I had been wearing a hat I would have taken it off to their ability to tail a guy like me without being spotted. I thanked the stars that I hadn't been stupid enough to call on Marge.

"So this TMU – tell me about him."

I had already told Rose Morton, once upon a time. Maybe she'd done the sensible thing and put it down to my unfortunate sense of humour – that and the drugs they'd been piping into me.

What was I getting myself into? What *could* I tell him? That TMU's the guy who's making all this up? The geek animating us freaks across so many pages of pristine A4?

They got out some rope and tried to make me uncomfortable. Then they worked on me. It was the kind of work they liked, with a lot of questions but a lot more fist. After a particularly intense bout of one-sided violence, we spent some quality time on the subject of TMU, and I ended up telling them the truth. I had no choice: they didn't believe anything saner.

They didn't believe the truth either.

"Oh, come on," I said, best as I could through the swellings around my mouth. "I tell you that you're all just made up names on bits of paper, players in a cheap drama to distract people in the real world from their daily grinds…and you can't swallow it? What's the matter with you?"

The mayor delivered a fancy speech about me not doing any swallowing for a while if I didn't stop messing with his head. I was out of options. I'd lied, I'd told the truth. I started asking a few questions. General stuff like how did a series-character maintain his identity whilst undergoing a fundamental change to his character. When that got no response I asked what really happened to Nancy Tate and Trudi Tremain.

And why.

Jackson asked if I thought any of that was my business, and I said that it needn't have been but that he was making it appear that way.

And so we reached a deadlock. It was around then that he told me that my room had been saved for me, back at the Town Hall. That it might be time to head back.

It struck me that the underground labyrinth where the dark quarter of the council conducted its real business, was a bizarre place for Frank Miller to reach his final end, and that my hole made a lot more sense. Or maybe it didn't. Either way, if they finished me, how would the story continue? And if it didn't continue, who would be able to make any sense of it?

I suggested that perhaps he was being a little hasty. He asked again about TMU and I said I would make a deal. "Tell me what the hell's going on," I said. "And then I'll spill the beans."

I tried to make it sound like a good deal, something worth considering. Jackson reminded me that I was in no position to make deals. Yet I had stirred his curiosity, all the same. Maybe he had nothing to tell me, but if so he wasn't letting on. He wanted to know what I had and who could blame him.

He started spinning some stuff about lone rebels trying to undermine the civil-minded efforts of the new and democratically-elected mayor. I tempered my scepticism due to the soreness around my jaw and cheekbones. I still had the swallow-reflex intact, though I couldn't take down the stuff he was serving up. And he could see that, plain as day, though there was nothing much he could do about it.

I said, "You need to do better than that. If I'm going to be straight with you, I need some give and take. See, I'm confused. You let me walk out of my VIP lounge in that whorehouse that you call headquarters, let me drive all around the city. Were you keen to know who my friends are – who I'm talking to

– or is it like in the movies: give the sucker a smoke so you can tear it out of his mouth the moment it's lit? You could have given me the nicely-does-it treatment back there, instead of taking a risk coming all the way out here."

"Nice day for a drive, Frank."

"I don't think so."

He sniggered like an obese child. "So you think that I'm taking a risk, do you?"

"Somebody might have seen you come in. Why chance loose ends when you don't need to? Doesn't make any sense."

"Dear, dear," he said. "That poor brain working overtime, eh? We'll be choking on the smoke if you keep that up."

"Amateurish, don't you think? Using the same technique twice?"

"I don't follow."

"You used fire on the Tremain house, shit face."

His jowls dropped into one enormous, squashed-up grin. "I see what you mean. No, I was speaking figuratively, Frank. We're not going to torch this place." He started laughing. "That would be gambler's folly, you're absolutely right. I mean to say, people might add up two and two and come up with –"

"Forty-five and a half stone?"

I thought he was about to hit me again. After all, I was overdue another dose of fist according to the cheap green plastic clock on the wall. Instead he smiled. "You're a funny man, Frank – you know that? A very funny man."

"You should see me in the Chapeltown panto. So okay, I give up. Why let me go and then follow me here?"

He told his stooges to leave the room.

180

When we were alone, he said, "You interest me, you know that? Listen, we'll forget about this TMU stuff for a while. We can come back to that."

"Oh, it'll still be here," I said. "That stuff's not going anywhere."

He nodded, as if he had at last found a wavelength on which to fruitfully communicate. "Frank," he said. "I'm sorry about the rough business. But, well, I had to know what I was dealing with. *Who* I was dealing with."

"And you've cleared all that up now, have you?"

"Let's say...we've made a start. It's enough for the moment. You see, I think you're working for the wrong side. I think, when you know the full facts, you're going to want to…change your allegiance."

He looked around the room and grunted. "This TMU guy doesn't pay you a great deal for all the crap you take, does he?"

"Less than you'd imagine."

"Come over and work for me, Frank. The rewards are more in keeping with your experience and expertise. The world's a marketplace. You sell your wares at a price that the market will bear. It's not immoral to do that; it's what life's all about."

I wondered how he did that. I'd been thinking about the marketplace and now he was taunting me with it. It was either telepathy or else more games from TMU.

I was favouring the latter. I said, "Let me ask you something. Do you always imprison prospective employees? Give them the rough treatment first? Is this my interview?"

He sniggered. "That's an interesting way of looking at things. I like it. I like you, Frank."

181

"Aw, shucks."

"But don't get me wrong. I'm not sentimental when it comes to likes and dislikes. I can like a man in the morning and break his legs in the afternoon."

I said, "You're just a big softy. I bet a whole family of yours could be dead by sundown."

He sighed and his eyes hardened. It was like looking at the only pig in the pen. The one the others were too afraid to come in and play with.

I said, "If I worked for you, what would I do exactly?"

His eyes brightened again. "You would sign some papers, to begin with."

"Aren't those home movies you made earlier security enough?"

"The camera can be accused of lying, Frank. Written testimony, contracts *and* the movies – different matter altogether. You come on the payroll, you get the full protection of a council employee –"

"Same as Nancy and Trudi, you mean? I don't think so."

"Let me finish, Frank. Come on the payroll and see what the council's offering its top people these days. You'd be surprised. This authority's going places. Be a part of it. Be a part of the new Chapeltown. You can start by telling me all about your…previous employers."

"So it's back to TMU?"

"If you like. Look, I'm going to give you some time to think about it. The boys outside can get the contract forms in front of you inside a minute. I'll give you a few seconds to read over them. You could be relaxing in your uncomfortable armchair in less than five minutes, with all your pain and woe behind you."

"What about TMU?"

"I'm not a greedy man, Frank."

"Are you certain about that?"

"Nor an impatient one, either."

"Perhaps I got you all wrong."

"I fear that might be what happened, Frank. So listen. How about I take the papers away with me and you tell me about your old boss in your own good time. I'm interested to know who this TMU guy is – what his racket is. But at the same time I'm willing to wait until you're feeling stronger, fresher, more relaxed. That's the kind of guy you'll be working for if you come over to me. See, I know people, Frank. I know how to get the best out of them. I get you to feel secure, feel good about yourself, and then we can really talk, you know, man to man. In my organisation we put people first, it's the only way. What do you say, Frank?"

I said, "I can't believe that I didn't see the ad."

"What ad's that, Frank?"

"The one looking for more goons to join the Chapeltown Mafia."

"You really are a funny man, Frank."

"I don't see you laughing."

"I'm laughing on the inside, Frank. But I need to know your answer and I need to know it now."

"What happened to all of that patience you were telling me about?"

He raised two eyebrows.

I held up two clean palms.

"What *can* I say?" I said. "Let's do it."

TWENTY THREE: THE MAYOR'S VERSION

It occurred to me as the pen hovered above the page, clenched between my fingers, that I might be signing my own death warrant.

It also occurred to me that I didn't have a lot of choice.

Our lovable mayor could spend a pleasant evening kicking me senseless and then arrange for a little 'accident' to round things off. But it wasn't what he wanted, at least I didn't think so. It wasn't really what I wanted either.

The way I saw it he wouldn't be putting in all of this time and effort if he'd already made up his mind to beat me out of existence. So this way at least I got to keep breathing air, even if it was the fictional air of Chapeltown, and growing more polluted by the hour. This way I got to buy myself a little time. Maybe buy TMU a little thinking time. A little cooling-off time, perhaps. For who was to say what might turn up while I made a show of playing the Fat Man's game?

The ink hadn't dried on the page when I felt the tell-tale crack on the back of my head. The next thing I knew about anything, I was waking up back in my old room in the subterranean bowels of the civic offices. It was the kind of nostalgia I could have done without.

I don't know how long I was in that half state of waking and drifting, but all the time I was reliving the past like I was coming to the end of the present. And every time I fell into sleep I was back in the library, reading over past glories, holding the beautiful bindings that held together the chronicles of Chapeltown's greatest detective hero, brushing the soft covers against my skin and wondering if there would ever again be one as great as Frank Miller.

Then I'd look again and I could hardly stand it – hardly stand myself at all. The conceited, self-centred arrogance. It was enough to make a grown man puke.

I'd given up; traded in living for the fantasy of immortality. I was a tortured soul, I tell you, watching myself in that stupid and sentimental dream, loving myself to bits one minute and hating myself with a passion the next. It was like there were two of me, two Franks.

Imagine that!

And one was gaining the upper hand – though the bookies around here wouldn't have liked it. The rank outsider – the Frank that wanted to honk up some of that burning acid in the guts – or else take that other Frank by the throat and give him one good crunch between the ribs to pull himself out of it – was emerging as the favourite after all.

Whichever side of me was going to win the fight, it was going to get dirty. That was the way the cards, the stars, the looking-glass jars were lined up.

It was no way to live.

I couldn't shake the feeling that somewhere in all of those volumes of glory, something was waiting to reach out and take me by the hand. The feeling grew. It took hold of old Frankie. And so, in that dawning of my eleventh hour, in that forlorn pit, I became convinced that a key lay hidden inside those books in the Chapeltown library. And if I could find it then the world might change and take me with it.

During one of my waking periods Thomas Jackson came in and spent some quality time with me. It wasn't the first time, though on the other occasions they'd been piping stuff in again and I hadn't been certain of exactly where my mutterings had taken us.

It was a tight squeeze, the two of us sitting on that bed together, and I quickly opted for the floor. He said that he fancied a movie and thought that we might watch it together.

Golden times.

Cosy.

We viewed some of my capers with Alice Coor and Michelle Spar and he made the suggestion that there were worse ways of treating a prisoner. If he was angling for a thank you, I had to disappoint him.

The film paused, just as I was getting to grips with Alice. It would have made an impressive still, the way all of that flesh was arranged, though I doubt it would have impressed Mr. Coor.

Jackson was eyeing me, grinning. "You must have some questions, Frank."

I couldn't lie. "Am I on the payroll already or do I have to work a week in advance?"

The laughter bellowed out of him. It was close to being infectious, but not quite close enough. "Frank," he said. "You're going to break my heart."

I looked at the still, frozen up there on the screen.

"Are you saying that you like me better than Alice? I always was photogenic, but I'm surprised to hear that I'm your type."

His mood shifted and I thought that perhaps he didn't like the insinuation. I wasn't too sure that I cared what he liked. "Frank Miller, heartbreaker," I said. "Why does it have to be that way?"

"Frank, listen to me. I'm a reasonable man."

"A what? Sorry. My mistake. For a moment then I thought you called youself – oh, I see now. What you really said was *unreasonable piece of -"*

"Frank, you really don't have an off switch for that mouth of yours, do you?"

I got to my feet and stood over his huge frame, sprawled out on the bed like it was Christmas afternoon in Chapeltown. "Look at it from my point of view, Fat Man. You hold me here, you take pictures of me, you let me go and then you come to my hole and make me sign papers. And then you bring me back here and none of it makes any sense. Yet you wonder why I'm not begging to kiss your fat corporate arse. Tell you what – if you want us to be great buddies, why don't we play a game together?"

"What game's that, Frank?"

"Oh, it's a good one. It's called how far can I bury my fist into that whale's belly of yours?"

He sighed. "You let the side down, Frank. But more than that you let yourself down. In another minute you'll be telling me all about this Man Upstairs again. All about being a character in a book."

"Will I? Would there be any point? We've been there once, maybe even more than that, as far as I can recall. You didn't believe it then and you won't believe it now."

"*The Black Widow*," he said.

I felt the air trap itself in my lungs and wrap around my heart like an anchor finding a rock. "What was that?"

"TMU always set things up well in advance. Even in *The Black Widow* there was talk of Chapeltown having an elected mayor."

"How would you know about that?"

"I've been to the library, Frank. I've read the books."

"There was no mayor in the books."

"Not in name. Typical of a leading man, failing to notice the minor parts adding *texture*. Chapeltown's been talking of electing a mayor through more than half a dozen of what you like to call the *Frank Miller Mysteries*."

"You're full of baloney. You've never been inside a library in your fat stinking miserable life. You don't know what a book is. If you can't eat it or hump it - whatever you've got, you've got from me."

"That's rich, Frank, coming from you."

"Wait a minute…"

"Try it, Frank. Give it a go, buddy."

"You're saying – you *know*?"

His grin grew like a stain, as carnivalesque as the Town Hall in a Halloween storm.

"*I know, Frank.*"

Laughter followed, as carnivalesque as the grin.

"Go on, Frank. Ask me a question."

"What drugs are you pumping into me? Why don't you end it here? To hell with anything making sense, why doesn't he set you loose to carve me up and give the finger to rhyme and reason?"

He got up off the bed. "That's some speech, Frank. Now I can see why he uses you for his leading man. Listen, I want to tell you something, but you're going to have to sit down on the bed because when you hear it your legs are going to give way."

I pointed at the screen. "Get rid of that first."

He clicked his fingers loudly and the image on the screen faded away.

"Okay," I said. "Serve it up."

"I really would advise that you take a seat first."

188

"They're all taken. That belly of yours doesn't leave a lot of space in a room this size."

"Have it your own way, Frank."

He told me how he woke up that morning, suddenly aware that he was a corrupt villain in a story. Said it like it was the damnedest thing imaginable. "I was running a crooked town, Frank, and it was the girls from a care agency who were doing most of the outreach work, getting into the homes of the voters and working into every thread of the society from deep within."

"Is that a fact?"

He told me that he was running the town using the carrot and stick method: sex and fear. The town was ideal, having no links whatsoever with any outside world.

"Strange thing is, Frank, that it never occurred to me that there even was an outside world. I was simply who I am, doing what I do, and I never questioned any of it. Then the revelation comes, and the whole thing seems preposterous. Nothing adds up. And I find out that I'm just the villain anyway; just a fall guy. I act mean, I threaten to turn Chapeltown into Sodom and Gomorrah, just so you can come along and rub my face into the dirt and be the hero and get the girl. The end of the road for the Mayor of Chapeltown, a character brewing since *The Black Widow* broke the records. All that building up and I get paid off in one book. Then you ride on with your bottle and your broad and I'm left as a mere footnote in the glittering career of Frank Miller. Doesn't seem fair, does it?"

I was trying to digest it. I'd had easier times digesting Chapeltown lobster Mexican style. I said, "So if you know, and I know – how many others?"

He shook his head. "Just the two of us, Frank."

189

"You're lying. That's the twist this time, isn't it? Every character in the book knows, but I'm the only one who doesn't know that they know."

"Hey, you know something?"

"What?"

"This has to be some of the best dialogue in the entire series. I'll be huge –"

"You're huge now, and ugly with it."

His laughter shook the room.

"Frank, come on, be reasonable: finish the scene. We're one short of completing your movie. I reckon TMU is firing on all cylinders here. We're nearing the end. We've got you, we've perplexed you. Our mystery has defeated you. My explanation has blown you out of your mind. It's all for glory, Frank. We want to live, and we want to oust the hero along the way. All we need is a final, dramatic scene and TMU's masterpiece is *in the can*."

A light blinked on in my head, then went out again. I said, "You're telling me he planned it this way from the beginning?"

Jackson frowned. The light tried to come back on, but it was struggling against a sea of black. I watched him hesitate, then pick up the rhythm again.

"How else could it be, Frank? He made us aware, didn't he – me same as you. The man's a storyteller. He can do anything. He can break all rules, all laws. He has no moral code to live by here in Chapeltown. Whatever rules exist, he makes them. You think I'm the villain – what am I compared against the one who made me? The one who *cast* me?"

The light in my head was feeble, yet it still registered a presence.

He reached into his jacket pocket. "You're going to love this part, Frank."

190

"Why do I doubt that?"

He took the papers out of his pocket and showed me what I had put my name to. My agreement to leave Chapeltown or else find my final resting place beneath the dirt of the city.

"We all got together, Frank."

I'd located the light again, but its glow was too weak to read anything by.

"We petitioned TMU to have you killed off."

"You did what?"

"Everybody in Chapeltown signed the petition – and let me tell you, Frank: that petition was long enough to wipe the arses of a field full of Chapeltown porkers with bacon poisoning. And we took that petition to TMU."

"Is that right? A moment ago you told me that we're the only two who know about TMU."

"So I lied, Frank. It's what I do. A man in my position doesn't have time to mess about with the truth."

"I can believe that. It may be the first thing you've said that I can believe. So okay, I get killed off. Then what? What's he got without Frank Miller?"

"Everything."

"I'm not following..."

"It's where TMU comes into the story, Frank. Comes down out of the clouds."

"Nice."

"Oh, wait 'til you hear the best part. TMU becomes the voice *telling* the story. His story all along. The puppet master out from behind the curtain. Isn't it exquisite?"

"I can think of better words to describe it."

A look of victory was filling out the creases of his bloated face.

I couldn't stand it. Had to do something. I glimpsed a loose thread and I took hold of it and yanked at it. "So you put all this into his head, did you?"

His face clouded over and in the gloom of it I glimpsed the light deep within me, starting to burn again. As bright as hope itself.

"How could you do that, Jackson? How could any of us – even an *elected mayor* - influence the thoughts of our creator?"

His confusion was glorious. He tried to hide it, but acting wasn't his strong point. His best work was clearly done behind the camera, not in front of it. A moment had arrived; a pivot, the hinge on which the whole thing would swing, one way or the other.

In the end it always comes down to confidence.

I knew, by instinct not intellect, the value of a poker-face. And I held that poker stare right into his fat, dark eyes. "No," I said. "No possible way to influence him. He decides - decides everything. We're just the pawns. We act out what he has already written."

The fat smile was dripping off his face, and the smell coming from it made my stomach heave. Still I held my stare. "Are you the sickness?" I said.

He shrugged. "How would I possibly know that?"

I was sensing blood when suddenly he brightened. "Hey," he said. "You know what this is?"

"Tell me, Fat Man."

"It's the calm before the storm, Frank. I'm going to leave you alone for a while, so you can have your final big idea. A way of saving yourself. A way of turning it around even at this late hour. Then we'll have the scene to end all scenes. The readers will get all the regular excitement, but this time they're in for a little extra."

"They deserve it," I said. "Paying good money to have to listen to all that bullshit. They like their heroes out and about, not holed up in the Town Hall."

"You kill me, Frank, you really do."

"Somebody should, and quickly."

"You've got it all wrong. In this book TMU pulls the carpet right out from under them. They won't know what's hitting them. Those many rules will be breaking that the mere inconvenience and frustration of having a detective holed up down here for a few chapters will seem like *nothing*. They'll be turning the pages so fast that the books will burst into flames. And then TMU will descend into the pages, just like I told you. And he will become the voice. I tell you, Frank – it's just going to blow their minds."

"Books bursting into flames, eh? Let's hope TMU's wearing his asbestos pants. The readers too, by the sound of it. Every copy coming free with a bucket of iced water to sit in when the thing finally gets going."

"You're funny."

"So they tell me."

"So here's something that'll appeal to that sense of humour of yours. TMU's sickness was nothing to do with the critics, or the pressures of writing – it was you, Frank. You were the sickness. He couldn't get your voice out of his head. You were meant to be a joke, my tired old friend, and then you started to take over. Your cynicism almost destroyed him, and it would have done if I hadn't stepped in."

"Is that a fact?"

"You've lost it, Frank. You lost it a long time ago."

"What did I lose, exactly?"

"Just about everything."

"Oh, come on. That just won't do. You have to be a little more particular."

"Okay. You lost your saving grace. Your wit, your charm. Your sense of humour. You give it but you can't take it. You were depressing him to death, same as you were depressing everybody else. Your time's up, pal."

He got up from the bed and crossed the room. Opening the door, he stood looking back from the threshold. "You're not laughing, Frank."

"I'm thinking about it, though."

The door closed behind him.

He was right. I had nothing to laugh about.

I'd been a whisker away from unravelling him. But he'd grown beyond what could be contained by mere words. He'd been feeding on this town for too long and too greedily to be overturned by wit alone.

I had to find my ending…

TWENTY FOUR: WAITING FOR THE BIG ONE

Jackson came back in like he'd forgotten something. He sat down next to me, almost tipping me into his lap, then placing a hand big enough to play golf out of onto my knee.

He squeezed. "Figured it?" he said, smiling. "I reckon you must have because you're a Big Shot Detective and nothing evades Frank Miller for long. I've read the books, Frank. I knew from the beginning what I was up against."

I said, "I think the bed's about to break and I was hoping to catch five before I turn in for the night."

His hand moved from my leg and I felt the relief of the weight lifting.

"Come on, Frank – what have you come up with? Don't keep me in suspense. You're a resourceful guy. No, let me guess a minute. You pull some bizarre card out of the deck, some piece of worthless information that no-one in this town or any other could care a damn about, and you hit me with it and I go down. Just like that. Then the long-legged bimbo walks in and you walk with her out into the sunset. Is that the great turnaround that you've been working on, Frank. Is that the best you can do?"

I said, "You're taking a risk, giving away your best ideas like that so cheaply. If I had a pen I'd write it down and start a new series with you as the hero."

"So you've got nothing, is that what you're saying, Frank? Not even some desperate scene that wouldn't impress a mentally challenged, oh, I don't know...turkey?"

"If you keep coming out with all these great lines I'm going to insist that you stop right there until I'm in possession of some writing equipment."

"You're still a funny guy when you want to be, Frank."

"So why is nobody laughing? Look, you want to know what I've got in mind, I'll tell you. I'm still working on it. I'm a perfectionist, see. I don't just have to win – I have to win in style."

"Well, Frank, that's as may be. But let me tell you this: you'd better not spend too long working on this great plan of yours, because time's in short supply as far as you're concerned."

"I'll bear that in mind. And by the way, the long-legged bimbo and the sunset are on the right lines, but you forgot about the mandatory whisky. It's details like that that are going to be your undoing."

His face fell into the shape of a laugh, but no laughter came out of it. He was too busy making himself look smug. "I want to show you the movie, Frank."

"Director's cut?"

"I have to warn you, though –"

"It's not an eighteen certificate?"

" – I don't want you to be disappointed. The movie's not complete. There's the little matter of the final scene."

"There's always something, isn't there?"

"We're planning to shoot it later. Let's see what we've got so far, shall we."

"Yes, let's..."

The screen came to life and the title shone across the room:

Frank Goes to Market.

"See the levels on which that title operates, Frank? I want TMU to use that title, too. *Frank goes to*

196

Market in a big way because this book's going to break all records. And *Frank goes to Market* because he finally becomes what he's been destined for all along."

"And what's that, if you don't mind me asking?"

"*Dead meat.*"

I said, "Sorry to interrupt, but that's a bad habit?"

"What's that?"

"Talking in italics."

"I'll try to bear it in mind, Frank."

"You do that."

"But let me continue. Because you're going to like this."

"I doubt that."

"You see, *Frank goes to Market* like the bloated pig, all fattened up - in your case, on women and whisky."

"Okay, I'll give you that one. I'm trying to cut down, though. Didn't you hear – it was my New Year resolution."

"Frank –"

"I know – I'm a funny guy. I think you might have mentioned that already."

"So what do you think of the title, then?"

I said, "I hope you're not going to keep this up and ruin the film."

And so the story unfolded.

Town Hall style.

With the opening scene I saw why they'd temporarily let me go: footage of the PI in his hole - how else could the film start? Subtitles made no secret of what was to follow:

A tale of love and blackmail.
Extortion at the highest level.

197

The mayor, a bad, *bad* man, and no attempt to conceal it; the monster making a brief cameo early on, his presence looming over the movie despite him being off-screen for most of it. I was in love with Michelle Spar. Then I blew it. They kept in the scene back at her house, with the fatal mention of Trudi Tremain. Alice Coor, Rose Morton, the living corpse in the bed and Jan his care agency lover – all there.

The man in the bed had undergone a remarkable transformation, though, and later in the film I witnessed acts of depravity performed by him that would have been impossible for the poor, emaciated creature I thought I had stumbled upon. Some of that stuff would have been impossible for a trained gymnast with a rabbit's heart.

They tried to throw in some vampire hokum, the guy biting the neck of the increasingly ambiguous Jan to freshen up his appearance. Jan, incidentally, had an impressive bosom, as it turned out, and had tortured me with it during my incarceration. She also, as it turned out, had a full complement of meat and two-veg. I wasn't shedding any tears during the fantasy sequence when they burned her at the stake.

My whole life since taking on the case was on that screen, with one omission.

Marge.

I wondered why she had been spared. Prayed that she had been.

I watched Jackson slugging my chops back in my hole. It hurt all over again, and I felt the ghosts of my fictional bruises starting to play around once more over the bones of my face. And then I was being tortured by Coor and company, but the orgy of drugs was now explicit; no gases seeping beneath the door, rather a host of substances taken willingly by a Frank

Miller too far gone to care less where the dividing line between reality and madness lay.

The incomprehensible plot had been reduced to childish simplicity as it rammed home its central message: that crime does pay, after all. And that once in a while, a guy as trim and good looking as Thomas Jackson comes along and tears the laws of morality to the ground, and has the public at large baying for more.

The girls from the care agency were fleecing the poor and vulnerable of Chapeltown, then filming them in acts of appalling degradation and threatening to expose the evidence unless relatives paid to see the reels burnt. By the end of the film, everybody in Chapeltown had been touched by the scam and become conspirators to the silence.

And against this, the one tiny house of resistance.

The Tremain house.

The film paused. "Not enjoying the movie?" said Jackson.

"I've seen better."

"Keep watching, Frank. What you're seeing here is your standard revolution movie. Out with the old, in with the new. One corrupt society replaced by a fresh one. The oldest story in the book. See, Trudi Tremain had some noble credentials, but she was also the biggest hypocrite you could ever meet. She just wanted to take a different route to get her slice of the pie, yet she had the nerve to dress her motives up as being somehow purer than anybody else's. But I reckon that made her perfect for a fallen detective like you, what do you say?"

I was with Trudi, down by the stream. They shot it so beautifully it made me want to spill a tear. Only the fat presence of Thomas Jackson prevented it.

They were on to us. We were fugitives, threatening the revolution and everything that stood to be gained in the new Chapeltown order. We had to be stopped.

The scene of the fire was breathtaking. I could feel the heat as the timbers fell and the brickwork crumbled like so much film-set cardboard.

He froze the action again. "Thought about ending it there – it's such a fine scene, don't you think? But you need a scene of your own, a showdown – so how about it? Just you and me, Frank – can you wait any longer?"

"Not unless you've any more of this crap to show me. And I still haven't had my popcorn."

"What a guy! But I'm afraid we're going to have to miss the refreshments."

"Wouldn't you just know it!"

The house lights came up. I clapped. "Planning a general release? You can't fail with this one."

"Got it in one, Frank. A certified winner. When it's finished, TMU watches it and falls in love with himself all over again. He sees what he is capable of – what he *believes* he is capable of. He types it out like he's become his own secretary, though it's still his name on the book jacket.

"But I can live with that, Frank. Because he has given me life and I owe him one. But in the pages, where it really counts, I rule like a god. The way you used to, but much more fun. What's on the outer cover – why should that concern us, Frank? Life is on the inside. Always was, always will be."

He got up from the bed. "Rest," he said. "You want to look your best for your big parting scene, don't you?"

When I didn't respond he put on a look of grave concern.

"You can't argue with the camera, Frank. The camera never lies – haven't you heard that one? It's all there. And with a careful tweak here, an edit or three there, we'll have the definitive Frank Miller all ready to meet his public. All we're doing is telling the truth about you, Frank. Revealing that the one responsible for every evil that ever came to Chapeltown, happens to go around in the disguise of a detective whose day of reckoning has just about come. Time for a new hero, Frank. And yes, you're looking at him."

He stopped talking. It was a good sound. Then he started again. "You look confused, Frank."

"As a matter of fact I am. Ever heard of continuity?"

"What are you saying?"

"The film starts with you portrayed as the evil mayor. And in fairness, I think you got that part nailed down. I'd say you were just about perfect."

"Thank you."

"My pleasure. But then for no apparent reason, and without any explanation, suddenly I'm the bad man. If I didn't know better I'd have to say that what you've got up on that screen is a perfect representation of the mind of TMU."

"Thanks again, Frank."

"It's not exactly a compliment. Can't you see – there's no logic to it. It's random. Meaningless. Tell you what, though."

"So tell me."

"I'm willing to take over as director, executive producer, leading man and ultimate hero – but on one condition."

"See you later, Frank."

"But you haven't heard my terms yet."

The door closed behind His Fatness and my bright lights of earlier came back only in memory. And all they did was illuminate the depth of my stupidity. Miller and Jackson, the Laurel and Hardy of this 21st farce, had one thing in common. We both knew that TMU was ill, seriously ill. Ill in the head, of all places.

To save me, to save Chapeltown and the people in it, I had to save TMU. If the darkness swallowed him, then it swallowed all of us –

- *and that included Marge.*

Could be she was already getting a knock on the door: Jackson telling her to come straight away if she hoped to save Frank Miller.

If she had any sense, she would close the door in his face and close that chapter of her life for good. Except that things weren't so straightforward any more in Chapeltown. Marge might be sick and tired of my adolescent games, but she wasn't the kind to give up on a friend, no matter how badly he was treating her.

And I wasn't about to give up on her. As far as the general population went, I could have lived with their demise. The town was just about rotten to the core and always had been.

But when TMU created Marge he changed everything.

It just took me a little time to realise it.

Now I knew the order of the day. Do it third for Frank Miller, second for the likes of Trudi Tremain, noble but misguided Trudi, but do it first for Marge.

It was good heroic thinking, and it would look right enough on the page. But it was no more than sharpening the pencils and straightening the back-to-school kit when I ought to have been getting on with the nailing of Thomas Jackson.

I turned my focus back on TMU. The lunatics he had created were about to take over the asylum; the madness creeping over Chapeltown like a shadow that no-one, least of all its most famous detective, had seen coming.

I had a glowing moment of insight. Or insanity. I gave myself the benefit of the doubt. The doctor instinct – the soldier on the field of battle gripped by the urge to tend to the wounded, the dying. To heal our creator - how heroic was that! A course of battlefield antibiotics made up and sent over the top. And an army of psychiatrists.

I was close to breaking point.

Close to conceding defeat and hoping that the end would come soon and come fast.

Was the whole shooting match worth saving? *Was it?* Damn the series. Damn Chapeltown and damn Frank Miller. If it wasn't for Marge I could close my eyes and be done with it all. But Marge could not be taken out of the equation. Marge *was* the equation. TMU had created her and in doing so he had turned the universe inside out. If Marge was spared I could bear anything.

Nothing lasts forever, not even stories from a sacred pen. Like the living, you have your day and then are gone like so many bones turned dusty. But why should she be spared? What better way to reduce me, torture me, prepare me for the final ending?

I held the thought, and then I tried to obliterate it. If TMU caught on, then Jackson was bound to, and Marge was done for, one way or another. Consigned to form a part of my farewell scene before taking her own place before the scaffold.

It was winking in the corner of my eye. A light, not bright and blinding like before, but this time pure and clean...and absurdly simple.

The thought in TMU's mind. The idea in the drawer.

I had no recourse now to sleep. I was too shattered to sleep. A condemned man – how *can* he sleep? And if he did catch a minute or two, what could he dream about but death and finality? Or, worse still, blue pyjamas that he might never look upon again.

Sleep might condemn Marge, if my careless thinking had not done so already. But I needn't fear sleep for it would not come now, so close to the finale. I closed my eyes and focused on the drawer. And the inside of my head became a palace of moving pictures that would beat the trousers off *Frank Goes to Market*.

My eyes opened, in more ways than one. The ceiling above me was out of reach and the ground beneath me solid concrete. If I started on the wall I might be through to reception in around thirty years.

The door was key, so to speak, but the answer lay not in breaking it down and not in picking the lock. The real key lay in who came through the door.

I didn't have to wait long to find out.

TWENTY FIVE: A LAST VISIT TO THE PALACE OF THE MIGHTY

"Playtime, Frank!"

My fist caught Alice Coor square in the chops the moment she came through the door. I planted it hard enough to take her down, but not hard enough to take her out. It was not in my nature to tow a dead weight through the bowels of the Town Hall.

I dragged her to her feet and pulled her out of that dungeon, a hand staying firmly at her throat. It took about five seconds for the first guard to arrive on the scene. He came complete with a gun that was pointing straight between my teeth.

"Drop it," I said, "or I squeeze."

I applied a little pressure to Alice's throat, producing a garrotted squeal that was hard on the ear. He looked at Alice and she nodded. The gun fell to the floor.

"Move back," I said. He hesitated. I let a little pressure off Alice's throat, just enough to let her tell the guard to move his "stupid fucking arse back."

I picked up the gun by the barrel and swiped the butt of it across his skull. He went down fast.

With the gun against Alice Coor's head we met little resistance and soon we were heading through the corridors where the day to day people walked, trying to mind their own business, despite a man dragging a woman along with a gun pressed to her temple.

"It's not as bad as it looks," I quipped, moving along the final stretch towards the daylight. "This is just a routine drill in case of a terrorist attack."

I think that some of the zombies moving along that passageway might even have believed me.

Outside the daylight was clearly on its last legs. I had no problem with that. Night time was Frank Miller time, and God help those who tried to take me in the darkness.

We moved out into the fading light, Alice doing a tiresome line in, "You'll never get away with this," and me responding with my own line in, "Just keep watching and try keeping that stupid mouth shut."

I took her about a mile from the Town Hall buildings and in the gloom of an alley I moved the gun into my left hand and gave her the second and final instalment from my right. This time she went down and stayed down. Nothing fatal – I'm not and never have been that kind of guy. Call it a weakness of mine. I'd measured out a shot that would keep her quiet long enough. I didn't need blood.

Tucking the gun into my waistband, I made my way to the Tower of Babel. Likely it was the first place they would think of, but what mattered was that I got there ahead of them. There were no other cards left to play.

TWENTY SIX: FRANK GOES TO MARKET

I was back amongst the filing cabinets, taking out manuscripts until they littered every surface, turning the floor into a carpet of story.

These were not the finished books I had looked through in the library, rather draft versions full of scribbled corrections and suggested alterations.

Where the real gold lay.

I picked out *The Black Widow*. The black-ink copy, a later draft by the look of it, made not the slightest mention of mayoral elections or Thomas Jackson. Yet he was there all the same. A pencilled asterisk, to begin with. A suggestion, in parenthesis: that a scene needed fleshing out. Background and texture but nothing more.

I found an earlier draft of the *Black Widow*. Here the strokes were much bolder. Jackson showing through more clearly, though still embryonic. The earliest draft I could find showed the clearest signs of all that a major character was in development. Strange, I thought, how subsequent drafts had toned him down, as though TMU had been fighting against the character's development. As though TMU already had intimations of where this new character might one day lead, threatening Frank Miller and threatening the series.

I took out another manuscript, an earlier version of the follow up to the *Black Widow*. The idea was beginning to take hold now. There was even a name, though still nothing particularly ugly about the character. Again, notes had been added into the margins. 'Thickening required'; 'texture.' Little things getting out of hand, and growing into bigger things turning nasty. Sloppy writing and half-baked ideas opening up strange gates leading into ghost roads. And the earlier the draft, the stronger the Jackson character.

Like light going backwards into darkness.

TMU had started losing his mind. The price he paid for creating the best work of his career? Perhaps. So okay, the jury's still out on that one, maybe. Yet for what it's worth, here's my take: TMU was covering up the madness represented by the Jackson character by diluting him in the 'finished' versions of his books. Fighting a battle on the inside that kept spilling out onto the page. Editing it out – but it kept coming back.

I could have trudged on through those endless drafts, but that kind of detective work, methodical and slow, was the prerogative of the old Frank Miller. And those languid days were long gone. The reader didn't want to settle down with an idea anymore; the reader wanted a barrage of incident, fast-talk and twists.

A new clock was ticking and with increasing urgency.

I left the filing cabinets and went for the secret drawer. I took out the death warrant with my name on it, and ripped it into shreds. Then I took a clean piece of paper from the drawer above, and a pen from the desk, and wrote:

FRANK GOES TO MARKET

Remember the phrase? You rang me up to ask about it. You've lost your way and need direction to finish the story. So try this.

Frank Miller looks into Tate's murder, uncovers a dirty racket run from the council offices by the elected mayor. But the case is a red-herring from the beginning. The real story is about you getting ill, for

208

which I'm partly responsible. I was stuck in my ways, couldn't change.

You can't live forever as a parody of someone else's golden age. You gave me life back by handing me the reins and for a while it worked. But you weren't in charge any more, and left to my own devices I became the child in the toyshop with no plans to move on.

Another rut full of women and whisky and corny as a spinster's feet.

But I'm not blaming you – you were ill and still are. Under pressure from your public, publishers, critics – you let your delusions take the shape of Thomas Jackson and you were prepared to go with just about anything.

You had a vague notion that I had become morally corrupt, and that 'elected mayor' had something to do with a guarantee of integrity. You were wrong on both counts.

So this book's about healing.

I'm changing and it's better than a rest – it's the cure.

You kill off a BIG character in the climax, but don't make it Frank Miller, don't sacrifice the series along with your career and don't let Chapeltown go to hell.

The twist isn't the death of the hero it's his salvation. Frank doesn't die, he changes.

You've given him Marge and at last he has something to fight for. You put her there at the start of the book, because you had big plans. Big plans for Frank. But then the sickness took over. It took over in the shape of a fat man who will swallow you whole if you let him.

He railroaded you and he will drive you out of your mind before he's finished.

Remember this: you created Marge for a reason. You created her to save Frank from what he was becoming. But then you lost faith and turned down the wrong street. And Jackson was waiting like a fever growing on the brain.

And okay, so it's a lousy outline, but I'm not the writer, remember. I'm just the gumshoe. I can't see how to turn this damned thing around, but I know there's a way to do it. I know YOU *can make it work.*

For what it's worth, I know this thing has to end outside the Town Hall. I keep going back to the Black Widow. The man who would be mayor, out there on the steps, pulling in votes. The dark seed that grew out of giving me consciousness. Who in hell knows how these things work? But they do, sure enough. You opened my eyes and one day I saw the results of what you'd done.

Jackson.

The key lies there, on the steps of the Town Hall. I know it, you know it. It's just the way it is.

I'm going to have to throw all my chips onto one number.

And rely on faith in my creator after all...

The door to the office flew open.

Jackson walked in.

I pulled out the gun.

"Put it down, Frank. We've got her. We've got Marge. She's waiting for you at the Town Hall."

TWENTY SEVEN: THE CONDEMNED MAN

They took me back.

This was the deal: confession, trial and execution – and for that Marge goes free.

I took it.

They didn't let me see her, not in person anyway. Instead they showed me the footage of her capture, showed them taking her into the Town Hall, down into the basement. Showed me her sitting on a bed in a room similar to the one they put me in. She looked scared, and why wouldn't she? No, she looked *terrified.*

When they'd finished with the film show I said, "Okay, let's do it. Let's get it over with."

"That's my man," said Jackson, slapping me on the back like I was a favourite son. "Now this is an important scene coming up. The one where I beat the shit out of you and get you nice and ready for your big confession. I want you to act natural, Frank. Play it from the heart. I want this to be your finest hour."

He shouted "Camera" and then he shouted "Action."

I looked above me. The ceiling was now made of glass, and a dozen lenses pointed down into the room, while one on wheels followed at the heels of the Fat Man.

He spoke like he was working from a script. "Okay, Miller, this has gone on long enough."

"I'll second that. TMU ought to be cutting to the chase."

"CUT!" he screamed, then eyeballed me, all steel eyes and gristle. He stepped back to the door. "Camera. Action." He came toward me a second time. "Okay, Miller, this –"

"Is the way we brush our teeth while we wait for TMU to uncap his fountain pen and cut the bullshit."

"CUT!"

His face was in mine. "You ruin this scene, Miller, and you'll be sorry."

"Sorrier than if I don't? Look, I've signed up to the public confession, the humiliation, the torture, the show trial and the execution – but don't milk it."

He went back to the door, gave me a last warning and then came at me again, using the same words.

"Cut!" I shouted, and the camera behind him died.

Another one lit and I looked into it. "You think Frank Miller's made of cardboard? You think he's incapable of change? I've learnt something these past few days, Fat Man, and I intend to share the knowledge."

I watched Jackson's face clench into a set of angry knuckles.

"My cynicism led to this, you once told me. I was turning into a cliché, replacing pastiche with parody with all my drinking and my womanising and my couldn't-give-a-damn-for-anything-or-anybody attitude. You woke me up and I'm grateful. Tell you the truth, I was getting sick of it myself."

"You don't know what you're talking about, Miller. You're out of your league."

His eyes were wild, and I could see that the brain behind them was unhinged.

"You didn't plot the death of me, Jackson. I suggested my own demise. The way I've been acting up these past cases – I was a strain on the reader and a boot in the pants to these downtrodden people who make up the town you're hoping to whip to death."

212

He was shaking his head. "Which joke shop did you buy this script from? You don't even sound like Frank Miller."

"Not the old Frank Miller. But you never heard about character development? You never heard about a fellow changing, becoming something that he promised to become a long time ago?"

"You? Make promises? Oh, Frank -"

"Go ahead, laugh. Because a one-dimensional blob can't defeat a developing character. The rules don't allow it."

"Whose rules?"

"The rules of story, pal. They're bigger than both of us."

It was my turn to do the laughing.

"The storyteller's back, Fat Man. Your kind's tough enough when it comes to the static, the cardboard man. But now I'm not so thin; now I'm a moving target and I'm talking the talk that this sorry saga's been about."

He staggered backwards, his jaw dropping. I sensed the cap coming off a pen somewhere; the dust cover leaving the word-processor keyboard.

"That's right, Jackson. This book's nothing to do with care agency corruption and mayoral perversion. Not really. This book's two things and this is your last chance to get it straight in that pig's head of yours before I send you to the slaughterhouse.

"Frank Miller's changing because he's sticking around for the long haul. That's the first thing for that pork head of yours to absorb."

I was taking a chance. I was throwing my aces down and hoping that a joker didn't count for double.

"Want to hear number two? Here it comes, ready or not. This book's also a love story, Jacko. Cute, isn't it? All the horseplay of a Roman orgy, and underneath a love story. I don't just get the girl this time, I get the real woman."

"A fine speech, Frank. The trouble is, I think you're forgetting that this *real woman* you're talking about is sitting on a bed similar to yours, and with a gun stuck to her head - just like the gun that you put to the head of Alice Coor, in fact."

"You must apologise to Alice for me," I said. "She mustn't take it personally."

"Oh, you'll get chance to do your own apologising, believe me. Before we finally put you out of your misery, Alice has requested a little private time with you."

I was almost out of time. I was hitting some sixes but it was all just words in the end. Jackson didn't even look dented by them. It struck me, looking into those necrotic eyes, that poking him with a stick whilst waiting for TMU to save the day was the worst kind of foolishness. I had to get the scene moving and keep faith that my maker might see fit to join the ride.

"Listen," I said. "This is a lousy scene. The two of us, here in this room, it doesn't cut the mustard. Why not kill a dozen birds with a single stone?"

"What are you talking about, Frank?"

"We need to be outside. We need to make this epic and for that we need to operate in a bigger space. Take the cameras out there with us, naturally."

"Go on," he said. "I'm listening."

"We need the drama of the Town Hall as a back drop. We need crowds, don't you see? We need the whole of Chapeltown assembled for this showdown. We combine my trial, my confession, my utter and public humiliation at your hands, and, finally, my execution. I will even beg for mercy if you like."

His expression suggested that he did like.

"I can hear the critics swooning, Jackson. I can see the house coming down. What do you say?"

His smile was almost genial. "You know, Frank, at times like these it seems almost a shame to kill you."

"Ah," I said. "I always knew that underneath all of that malice and psychopathic megalomania, there beats the heart of an old teddy bear."

"We can take it outside, Frank, that's no problem. We can get the town out there or else watching on TV– or both."

His eyes lit. Then narrowed. "What are you working here, Frank?"

The truth was that I was running on empty. Trying to draw TMU, getting him to see the merits in reaching down with that big, mighty pen of his and turning the Fat Man into dust and me into the hero. Yet I knew, without any doubt, that this scene had to take place. And that it had to take place out on the steps of the Town Hall, where it had all started, if I was to have any chance of saving Marge and saving the series.

"What am I working?" I said. "I'm trying to save the woman I love, that's all."

He shook his head. "You're up to something, Frank. What's in it for you?"

"Okay, so I'm a coward. You finish me quickly. That's the pay off."

"Why would I do that?"

"You want to be the hero, don't you? What's to wait for? Why waste your time tormenting me when you've a whole world to play with?"

He considered my words carefully. "Okay," he said. "Your death sets your girlfriend free, but for killing you quickly I want a full, public confession."

"You've got it."

215

He shook his head. "No, Frank, I don't think you understand. It's not enough any more to say that you have seen the error of your ways. You have to go further. You have to say that you have spent your career corrupting Chapeltown, trying to destroy it. That you killed Nancy Tate and Trudi Tremain so that you could pin it all on me. And then you have to tell them that I have come to save Chapeltown from the evil that is Frank Miller."

I shrugged. "It's your movie, Fat Man. Saves the expense of a fair trial, too. And for good measure I will even throw in the truth, the whole truth and nothing but the truth about The Man Upstairs."

"What's to tell, Frank? What's to tell that we don't already know?"

"Everything. And when I've told it, then you finish it, out there on the Town Hall steps. Like the gladiator that you are, you finish Frank Miller for good."

I saw the light shining like a bright star behind his eyes. There was something in there that he liked. There was a lot in there that he liked.

He thought about it for a minute, but only for the sake of appearances. It was written across his pork face that he had already decided.

"Okay, Frank," he said at last. "You've just made yourself a deal."

His face burst into a grin that could have scared every child in Chapeltown to death, if the town had any children to scare to death.

He held out a hand. "Shake on it, Frank."

I held out a hand of my own and felt the sweat of his fist soak into mine.

"You know something," he said.

"What's that?"

216

"You kill me, Frank. You really do."

"Aw shucks," I said. "Do you mean it?"

TWENTY EIGHT: THE NEW CHAPELTOWN

Disorientation was kicking in again. Day and night swapping around like TMU couldn't control the reality he was creating. He needed to get his act together. I could play my part – and I intended to. But without him firing on all the right cylinders the thing was doomed.

It was getting late in the day by the time everything was set up. The sun was low in the sky and there was an end-of-the-world feel outside the Town Hall when they led me out.

The crowd was vast. The cameras ready and pointing.

We stood, Jackson and I, on the steps of the Town Hall, just the way I had imagined it. The crowd was attentive though hushed and there was a crackle of electricity in the air. The scene that was to unfold would be transmitted live into every home in Chapeltown through the miracle of television. Nobody was going to miss it.

Jackson was wearing his chain of office over a dark grey suit. I had on my PI's raincoat, though no-one had thought to give it a dry-clean for my big night.

There was a microphone set up on the steps and Jackson put his face around it.

"I want to thank the people of Chapeltown for coming out this evening, and to thank those watching at home. You may know the name *Frank Miller.*"

There was a murmur, little more, coming off the crowd. I might have expected a stronger reaction, one way or the other.

"Frank Miller is a detective who works the streets of this town and has done so for a long time.

Some would say too long. As you may have noticed, things have been changing around here lately, and changing for good."

The crowd offered its first round of applause and Jackson milked it for a while before waving a fat fist to quiet them down.

"Well not everybody, it seems, embraces what we are doing here at the Town Hall. Not everybody recognises that we have the well being and happiness of every single one of you in mind as we begin to dismantle the old Chapeltown and give birth to the new vision."

Applause broke out again. They were really thumping and hooting this time. It had the unmistakable ring of inauthenticity about it. Jackson made a meal of quietening them down again, clearly loving every moment of adulation.

He took hold of the microphone, pulling it off its stand. "You know, when I took up this position. When you elected me, democratically, to shake up this town and turn it into something to be proud of. Well, people, I knew from the very start that there was one among us who would try to derail what we have set out to achieve."

He looked over at me. Directed the gaze of the crowd at me. "So please, let's give a big Chapeltown welcome to that man, our very own Mr. Frank Miller."

He handed me the microphone and a thick silence descended. I stood surrounded by a sea of silent hostility. If he had given the word; if he had merely clicked his sausage fingers, they would have been on me. That sea of misguided sheep would have unleashed the collective wolf within, then engulfed me and spat out the bones.

"That was some introduction," I said. "So how are you all doing tonight? I can't hear you. Frank says...HOW ARE YOU ALL DOING TONIGHT?"

The silence sounded locked in. Going nowhere.

"Okay, later I may finish with a song, but let me start with a story. Once upon a time there was a man standing on these very steps. A man without a name. A fat man. Screwing you for votes while I was out there nailing the *Black Widow*. While I was out there making these streets safe for you to raise your children, if you had any, this dark shadow of a man who would one day trick you into making him mayor, was starting his campaign, spreading his poison."

The assembled were keeping their silence, but there was a restlessness growing.

Did they want my blood so soon?

Couldn't they wait to hear me out?

"You may be wondering what exactly you're all doing out here tonight. I'll tell you. You're here to listen to a confession. About how this detective, this Frank Miller who you see before you corrupted Chapeltown, and how the mayor has come to save your miserable hides from the evil that is I. Well, I'm feeling generous. I'm feeling like throwing in a history lesson for good measure. Who knows about the *Black Widow*?"

Silence.

Restlessness.

"Isn't there a single one of you out there who's even heard of the *Black Widow*?"

I turned to Jackson. "You ever heard of the *Black Widow*?"

He shrugged.

"Is that a yes or a no, Fatso?"

He shrugged again. Then he held out a greasy fist. I handed him the microphone.

"Is it some kind of exotic spider?" he asked me. The crowd laughed. Then he handed the microphone straight back to me. "Let's hear some more about this *Black Widow*, Frank."

The silence descended once again, hostile and impatient, and I was getting tired of it. I said, "Do any of you out there read? Do any of you ever visit the library here in Chapeltown? It seems to me that your beloved mayor knows Jack Fucking Shit about the history of this town. For the record, the *Black Widow* was my thirteenth case. A masterpiece from the pen of The Man Upstairs."

The crowd gave not the slightest indication that they had a clue what I was talking about. It looked to me like they wanted to cut to the chase and see some blood flowing down those Town Hall steps. "Okay," I said, "so who remembers this little jingle:

The Mayor of Chapeltown
How did he win?
Seduced the women
And frightened the men."

Jackson took the microphone out of my hand. "Hey, that's catchy. I could use that for my next campaign. How much do you want for the copyright?"

The crowd were laughing again, clapping like a herd of well trained otters. A regular little circus he had going. Jackson handed the microphone back to me. I watched the otters turn back into a wolf in sheep's clothing as the fat ring-master positioned his fat head in an aspect of mock solemnity.

"Listen," I said. "All you need to know is this: Thomas Jackson here – this so-called *Mayor of*

Chapeltown – is nothing more than some cartoon slob subject to the whims of a deranged author."

That did it. That got me my first laugh of the evening.

I decided to go for broke.

"Jackson here is nothing more than a sickness that needs to be cured. And I'm that cure."

The laughter spread like fire through the crowd, quickly becoming something dangerously close to hysterical. I thought, with an audience like this every night, I could give up sleuthing and start a career as a stand up comedian.

It was time for the punch line.

"You see, folks, it all comes down to The Man Upstairs. It's time you knew the truth about him. He's the man who created all of this. The man who created Chapeltown, Thomas Jackson and every last god-forsaken one of you. Even - and I'm no longer ashamed to admit it – *Frank Miller*."

The laughter was building with every sentence. "Don't you get it? He's written all of us into existence. He is our author...and our god."

The laughter finally made it into full blown hysteria. It was pointless saying any more; they wouldn't have heard a word. I felt the microphone leaving my hand again, and heard the crowd begin to hush down as Jackson started to speak.

"So that's what we're up against, people," he said. "That's the measure of this man who stands before you, calling on your mercy here today. That's the measure of Frank Miller. He would spin you fairy stories and hide behind them. Why? Because it's easier to blame his shortcomings on some fantasy that he has dreamed up to escape his responsibilities to all you good people of this town. All of this hocus pocus about

222

The Man Upstairs – about any kind of supernatural force controlling our destinies – is the last desperate attempt by a washed up, fallen hero to save himself from the true and proper justice that awaits all men of evil.

"Frank Miller is about to be exposed for what he really is, and what he has been all along: a letch, corrupt and dirty in mind, filthy in body and spirit. An old and broken stereotype that this *New Chapeltown* of ours can do without.

"He is a curse upon the very behind of all you good people."

The crowd started to cheer and roar.

"There's a movie that you will all be watching – and watching very soon. A movie that tells the truth about Frank Miller. Because when it comes down to immorality, Frank Miller has no equal. What you are witnessing here this evening is the last scene in that film. What you are witnessing here today is the-man-who-would-be-king getting his just desserts."

Jackson was whipping up the crowd like only a merciless man of politics can, and they were sounding to me like a mob about ready to do the mayor's dirty work for him.

But Jackson still wasn't quite finished.

"The way forward does not lie in superstitious belief in some old god. In some *man upstairs*. The way forward lies here. In me. I can take this town where it needs to go. I can lead you into days of sunshine and plenty."

I was about ready to start wiping the tears out of my eyes. Some were already doing just that.

Jackson thundered on.

"I am the saviour. The man you voted for. I am everything you need and everything that you will ever need. I am the revolution and the life everlasting."

He paused. Turned to me. *Grinned.* "First though there is a price to be paid here today. And I think you all know exactly what I'm talking about."

He pointed a fat finger right at me. "Prepare to die, Frank Miller."

The crowd were baying for blood. *Mine.* It was nothing if not impressive the way Thomas Jackson could stir up a bunch of empty-headed simpletons.

"Actually, Frank, there's one more thing I would like to say before I set the dogs on you."

"Go ahead," I said. "I've booked the entire evening off."

"You see, good people of Chapeltown, Frank Miller here wanted to do a deal. He said that if I let him die quickly, and if I spared his *girlfriend*, he would tell us all about this 'man upstairs'. I say that for all the trouble he has caused – and for trying to corrupt our minds with all this fantastic hokum about supernatural forces and ancient gods – the deal is off."

The crowd hollered their approval. And Jackson stood there soaking it up, every last dreg. "I think we're almost done," he said at last. "But before we get to the bloodletting, I think we should indulge the great detective one last time. I think we ought to join in with that jingle that he shared with us earlier. What do you say, good people of Chapeltown?"

What *could* they say? They thought it was a great idea. They would have thought it a great idea if he'd told them that he was about to open up the machine guns on them. And so they all sang together, the whole damned lot of them, with Jackson leading.

The Mayor of Chapeltown
How did he win?
Seduced the women
And frightened the men."

"And again, good people."

And so they sang it again. And again. And - but you get the idea.

Jackson asked why I wasn't joining in. I told him that I once had a cross-eyed singing teacher and it put me off live performance for life.

When Jackson and his flock finally grew tired of the song - and it took them a while - he turned to me, looking about to deliver what I imagined would be the final address.

I was right.

"You're going to die like a mouse in the cat's mouth, Frank. Slowly and cruelly, because that's nothing less than a guy like you deserves. And as for your girlfriend...well, let's put it this way: I think hell's waiting. A *living* hell. There's no escape from this town, not for her, not for anyone. You're the exception, Frank. You get to leave because Chapeltown simply isn't big enough for the both of us. But Marge - that's a different story. She will enter that living hell even before you've finished screaming, and she will be personally overseen in all her misery by none other than...the Chapeltown Angels."

Jackson looked over to the far right of the crowd. "Would you like to come forward, ladies?"

I watched as the crowd parted like some old time Red Sea, and some familiar figures, all of them female, stepped out in front of the assembled masses.

Michelle Spar was there. Alice Coor. Rose Morton. There were others that I didn't recognise, but they all had the same look about them. Hard faced, sour and ready to inflict suffering at a moment's notice.

"Your girlfriend will be in good hands, Frank. The same as you were, once upon a time. But playtime's over. This time it's for real. I think we're done here. Let's bring it on."

TWENTY NINE: THE OLD FRANK RISES

Had TMU abandoned me? Had it all been for nothing? What was I expecting – to see Him descending from the sky, fighting the battle for me? In the end it all comes down to faith.

Faith and love...

He still had the microphone in his greasy fist when I went at him. He took a good one to the chin and then he took some more good ones to the rest of his over-sized carcass. My fists were blazing and it felt good connecting with bone and blubber like that.

He rocked a little but he didn't go down. I was expecting the crowd to be on me. Maybe they thought that the odds were so stacked against me. That this flurry on my part was nothing more than an annoying bug buzzing around the head of a living god in the last few seconds before it was squashed into the dirt.

Gathering himself like a human mountain, he came back at me, head down, charging like a bull – though still with a pig's face. It was not a pretty sight and I felt my stomach lurch and then twist a little.

Still I waited, stood my ground; didn't give way to the foibles of panic. (It takes nerves of iron and it's not something I would recommend that a beginner tries at home.) At the optimum moment I brought up my knee and took some of the rigidity out of his bacon chops. The crack must have sounded to the people above ground like the start of an earthquake. Chapeltown on the brink of apocalypse.

Jackson wiped the pain off his face and came at me like immortality depended on it. His fists were fast for a fat man, and he could dance too. And those are the qualities apt to bring out the best in Frank Miller. Qualities that had been allowed to get a little rusty, perhaps, over my last few adventures.

Literary experimentation had curbed some of the violence that came with my original conception and it was good to see that despite everything there was still blood running in my veins, and not merely a boldness that was all down to type-face.

After sinking a particularly deep fist into the belly of Thomas Jackson, and taking a piece of this town's sacred spleen back, I told the assembled that this one was for Trudi Tremain. When he crumpled, I went around the back and straightened him up with some rabbit punches to the kidneys that also had Trudi's name in the dedication. And then it was time to run all the way back around to the front, to add a few facial improvements in the name of a dear old lady and her kitchen table, and to the memory of those blessed unseeing eyes when I might otherwise have found myself compromised.

Still the crowd refused to make a move on me.

Did they know something I didn't?

Was Thomas Jackson indestructible – merely acting the part of a man who was taking a beating? Was I doing nothing more than winding up the queen in the wasps' nest?

Jackson kept on soaking up everything that I could throw at him, like the huge sponge that had soaked up all the poison leaking from TMU's brain over the years. And then I thought of Marge and everything went through the gears. As each blow struck home, something was happening. I could hear moans of pain coming from the front of the assembled, over to the right where the Chapeltown Angels were standing.

I took a moment from my labours. The groans of pain were spewing out of Coor and Spar and Morton as they watched the Fat Man going down and down and down. Every blow reduced those bitches, thinned them right out until they were on their knees begging me to stop. If Marge had been harmed I would never have stopped, not until my fists had become raw and the throats of the protesting few bleeding for mercy.

Jackson needed their adulation; without it he was nothing but a beached whale dying in the air, if minus the poetry and the tragedy.

As those final blows landed I was turning the scene into a song and dance routine. What a rhythm I was beating and what a mover I had become as I gave my public the blood-soaked waltz.

As the Fat Man faded I threw in a few on Nancy Tate's account, even though I had never met her. And a random assortment for any good people of the town that I was fast becoming proud of again.

The applause started slow but it quickly gained momentum. It was clear that Jackson wasn't getting up. That all it took to beat the Fat Man into the dust was one good man with two good fists and the will to take him on.

Faith is what it took.

And a soupcon of love.

The crowd were hailing their new hero. I was really their old hero, but this wasn't the time to start splitting hairs. I took their applause along with their fickle worship. I knew that being flavour of the week around here had nothing to do with integrity and everything to do with being top dog, no matter what your methods.

Today I was their saviour.

Tomorrow?

Tomorrow was another day and it would have to take care of itself.

They carried Thomas Jackson away on a door. The stretchers had kept ripping under the strain, sending him down onto his face for a series of unplanned meetings with the unforgiving Town Hall steps. So they smashed down the door that had once held me prisoner and they laid him flat on it to cart him off.

I thought it was a nice touch and I still do.

He wasn't dead, though. It wasn't the Miller way to see a man smashed to pieces and unable to live out a life of regret in some hole even more Spartan than a private detective's latest living quarters. It was a life for a life: Marge had lived and so Jackson could keep what was left of his own miserable existence on her account.

The triumvirate of women on the floor had ceased their collective hysteria, and were looking around bewildered, like they didn't know what they were doing out there. As though an exorcism had taken place and the demon had left them to gape in innocent confusion on a world turned upside down.

They blinked towards me, like butter wouldn't melt. I told them to get the hell out of town, secretly savouring the impossibility.

For them it would be an eternity on the run.

Exile.

The worst kind of death.

The police came down, a little late as usual. We gave them the evidence, though the editors Jackson had employed to complete his movie said they could do with a few hours to work over the last rolls of film and finish the job properly.

230

The boys in blue agreed to that, though they insisted on over-seeing the editing. I wasn't sure Chapeltown's finest would notice if it had been in anybody's interests to swap the whole thing for a copy of that movie TMU was always alluding to, and which I believe goes by the name of some broad, *Mary Poppins*.

It's what happened, anyway. And I've heard on good authority that the police department, in conjunction with a plague of Town Hall academics, have set up a working party for the next few years to study that same film and try to make sense of the entire episode.

There were a few arrests, for the sake of appearances.

The usual suspects, as usual.

I managed to get hold of the actual movie that Jackson had thought would destroy my reputation. The genuine footage. I have to say that it was not a great film, though it certainly had its moments. I kept hold of it purely for reasons of nostalgia, you understand, though I'm considering having the portrait of Jackson framed by the cheeks of Alice Coor's arse, cut from the print and mounted over the fireplace in my hole.

But all of that's another story and I haven't finished with the present one.

Sometime later, as the night that they carried the mayor away on a door hovered indecisively over the streets of Chapeltown, I left the Town Hall and made my way across the car park. As I climbed into the trusty old Cherry, I glanced back and saw, in that clear, star lit night, that the clown's grin had gone from the building.

I sat there for a moment, taking it in. And as I sat there I thought about my hole. Wondered if I had seen it for the last time. It seemed to me that I'd made a

231

case for some decent digs and to be honest I was feeling pretty confident that my pleas would not, this time, go unheeded. I'd stick with the wheels, though. You can change too much too soon and lose touch with yourself.

The jalopy was just fine. More than fine in fact.

Yet as I pulled off the car park I couldn't help wishing for a horse and sunset.

I pulled over at the burnt out wreckage of the Tremain house and wandered around the ruins that the council still hadn't got around to flattening. I knew about the power of the re-draft, and for a few moments I speculated on how far my influence extended. Could I, even now, persuade TMU to reconsider this part?

To let the girl and the old lady live?

Yet deep down I knew that was fantasy land, and fantasy land was not a place where a hard-boiled guy could live for very long.

I let the tears go and mingled them with a prayer. Two firsts for Frank Miller. I had some garage flowers that I happened to have picked up on the way, and I laid them down among the ruins and the memories. Then I got up, checked that I was alone, and got back in my car. I was changing, I *had* changed, but there was still only so much that could be accomplished in a single volume without giving the reader the idea that they had picked up the wrong book.

I looked back a final time, put my car into gear and gently let out the metal. And it was in that precise fashion that I headed towards Hill Street and the Honeywall Flats.

THIRTY: NEW PYJAMAS

I stopped outside the flats and stood at the roadside looking up. If I had thought for one second that I had played out my finest scene already - that the Town Hall had witnessed the best of Frank Miller - it had all been for nothing and would always amount to nothing.

But the better part of me, the changing part, knew that my finest hour was still ahead, waiting for me to claim it.

Standing outside Marge's door I had it straight. TMU was going to use all of it. It was the cure and he had taken it and come through. *His* exorcism; *his* purging.

The dozens of blows that landed on the foul body of Thomas Jackson had been the unleashing of the creeping sickness that had taken over TMU. It was spent. He was free of it. He was clean again. The destruction of Jackson had been TMU's scene.

And now he owed me mine.

Marge came to the door. She looked surprised to see me. For a moment she hesitated in the doorway, and I felt my faith getting ready to slip. Then the door opened wider and I followed her inside. "Still busy cleaning up the streets of Chapeltown?" she said, pouring out two large ones.

"I've knocked off for the night, Marge."

She looked up from what she was doing.

"Taking some time out," I said.

"The great Frank Miller? What about the plagues of evil out there? What about the beautiful women? Doesn't everybody need you, Frank? Don't they need you every minute of every day?"

A couple of sharp lines flashed across my brain, about saving her and Chapeltown from a fate worse than death at the hands of a messed up writer. But I let the thoughts go, let them shoot out like stars into oblivion. I had no need of them tonight.

"Are we going to drink those drinks?" I said.

"All in good time, Frank. I want to ask you a question."

She was looking good enough standing there in those old slacks she sometimes lounged around in. But I knew that she could do better. Even so I kept my mouth shut. I was walking into a comeuppance, and I could already feel the heat of it.

"I want your opinion on something I got from town today."

I shrugged. "Okay, go ahead."

I watched her disappear into the bedroom. My first thought was blue pyjamas. *She's gone out and bought herself a new set just for me.*

She came back out of the bedroom a lifetime later. The drinks were still in the glasses. She came out wearing pyjamas...*bu*t *not blue ones.* These were white. Soft and well tailored.

At first I thought that there must be some mistake.

She did me a twirl. "So, Frank – what do you think?"

I said, "I'm sorry, Marge. I've spent so much time lately thinking about the blue ones. It's going to take some time to adjust."

"You said you'd time now, Frank."

"And I wasn't kidding. I wasn't kidding at all, Marge."

She went over to get the drinks and then we chimed the glasses together. It was celebration time. As we drank together I looked at her hard, right in the eyes, trying to weigh it all up. *Would TMU let her retain the knowledge of all that had transpired? How would he play it?*

I looked at the blank TV screen. "When they brought you back here," I said. "Did you catch any headlines?"

She shook her head. "Nothing, Frank. Nothing at all."

I was raising my glass to drain it when she said, "Now you can ask *your* question."

"What question's that, Marge?"

"The one written all over your face."

I lowered the glass, and then I pointed towards the bedroom. "You think we might be more comfortable in there?"

She turned around and I followed her in. I was getting to like the look of those new pyjamas and didn't imagine it would take too long getting over the loss of the blue ones after all. We got comfortable on the bed and I started to pick her out of those Frank-teasers. She stopped me. "Haven't you forgotten something?"

Had I? It seemed to me I had everything I needed.

"Your drink, Frank."

"But –"

"You want to end the story in style, don't you?"

I looked at her.

"Something wrong?" she said.

"You know about me?"

Her smile was beyond wicked. A thousand miles beyond it.

"How long have you known, Marge?"

"Does it matter?"

I sighed out a long breath of sweet contentment. "Would it make you happier if I brought in the whisky?"

"Would it you, Frank?"

"Not particularly."

"Good," she said. "So what are we waiting for – violins?"

The whites came off like we'd been rehearsing all our lives. And when I placed the soul of Frank Miller back where it longed to be, I cocked an eye towards the ceiling for all those imaginary cameras, and let off a wink, Miller style…

The book came out and the rest, as they say, is history. More or less. Except that the book didn't come out, at least not right away.

When I reached that final scene with Marge, getting comfortable without the whisky and then without the pyjamas, I knew all I had to do was give it that timeless period before making a return visit to the library.

I was looking forward to pulling up a chair and getting stuck into the latest addition to the Frank Miller canon. I'd been through the old photographs, so to speak, and it was time to look at how my latest holiday snaps had turned out.

So that's what I did. I visited the Chapeltown library.

All the other books were there, all twenty of them, exactly as I'd left them after my last visit.

Twenty.

Not twenty-one.

I asked one of the staff and he was remarkably well informed. It seemed that there had been problems with the latest book in the series. I could have commented on that!

I kept my peace and he told me that the literary pages had been full of the story. He seemed surprised that I hadn't come across it myself, being so interested. I shrugged it off, said I was only interested in the books themselves, not all the politics that lay behind them. There was no reason for him not to believe me.

He told me the saga. Business was slow at the library that day and he didn't seem to have anything else to do. He took his time and didn't spare the details;

a man with a story to tell relishing the company of somebody who'd listen.

He told me about how the author had delivered the completed manuscript of the twenty-first Frank Miller mystery to his publishers, and how they'd suggested certain amendments.

"Amendments?" I asked.

"Sounded to me more like throwing the book down the pan and starting from scratch."

"That bad?"

"The author held his ground, though. Said he'd find another publisher. Reckoned he could get around contractual obligations by writing some other crap and offering them that. But he insisted that the Miller book remain intact and go to the first enlightened publisher who'd take it. Those were the words he used – 'enlightened publisher'. Got to hand it to him…"

"So what happened?"

"Well, the existing publishing company knew that the book would shift enough copies to make a decent profit, even if it had been written by the author's cleaning lady."

"Writer, is she?"

He didn't laugh. Who could blame him?

"They compromised. Some minor changes, but essentially the book will come out in its original form."

"Any idea about these changes?"

He shrugged. "I only know what I read in the press. I'm just a library assistant."

"And a good one at that."

I thought he blushed a little around the neck when I said that, and I had no wish to add to his discomfort.

I left it another timeless while before making my return trip to the library. In the meantime I took a small slice out of eternity to do nothing but reprise that end scene with Marge.

Last pages – you can't beat them.

It was just such a perfect way to finish and I couldn't seem to get enough of it. All the same, the time eventually came to go back to look for my coming of age tale.

The assistant was there when I arrived but the book still wasn't. He looked pleased enough to see me and I guessed that he was bursting with an update.

It seemed that I was right. "Still looking for Frank Miller?"

"You could say that."

"There have been developments, apparently."

"Did the cleaning lady get the gig?"

For the second time he failed to laugh at the joke and again I refused to hold it against him. He told me that the book was expected any day. The latest word in "literary circles" was that all parties had agreed the book's final form and that all that was left to do was get the printing rollers fired up.

"Any ideas yet on the changes?"

"Well, apparently the last thing to be agreed on was the title."

I took a breath. "The title? You wouldn't happen to know..?"

"I heard that the publishers wanted *The Mayor of Chapeltown*."

"They wanted what?"

A chorus of ssshhh kicked off behind me, and I turned to see a group of old ladies all pointing at the library sign advising patrons to keep the noise down. "Sorry," I said. "I don't get out like I used to."

"You don't like that title?" asked the assistant, who seemed a lot less concerned about noise than his customers.

"Do you!"

His head recoiled at the vehemence of my response, and the old ladies kicked in again with their hushing chorus. I smiled to placate him and whispered to placate them.

"Sorry," I said, "but I'm a big fan of the series. I hate to see a talented author throwing away his career on an ill-thought out title."

He still wasn't biting. "You don't think that title's a big mistake?"

He looked uncertain. Trying to weigh me up. "I haven't read the book yet, but the author certainly didn't like the title and I reckon he ought to have the final say."

"Damned right," I whispered, surprising myself. "And full marks for your tact and diplomacy. You will go far in this library. But let me tell you – for the record: that title stinks."

I didn't imagine he had anything else to tell me, and I was about to thank him for his time when he looked at me, nervously but determined, and said, "*Frank Goes To Market.* I read that's what the author wanted, but the company gave a flat refusal."

"Is that a fact? I could have lived with that, too," I said. "He got that one from me."

"Excuse me?"

"Oh, nothing. Just a series-character getting a little above his station, that's all."

He hesitated. I could see that he had the title ready on his lips, but wanted some assurance that I wasn't going to yell the place down or even physically attack him if I didn't like it. We looked at each other for

240

a while and then he evidently decided to take the risk. The old ladies had moved away and he must have worked out that the damage would be limited.

He coughed first, and then out it popped.

"*The Man Upstairs*."

I didn't say anything. I may have blinked a few dozen times and probably swallowed a dozen more for good measure. But the words were lost somewhere inside me. I heard him say, "Are you okay?" I heard those words, and I saw his mouth move, yet the two events appeared curiously out of synch. At last I heard the whispered echo come out of my mouth:

"*The Man Upstairs.*"

"You like it?"

Sometime later I made one final trip to the Chapeltown library. I had to get out from under Marge's feet and give her some space. Not that she was angling for that; after all it was like we were living in fairy-tale land, up in those Honeywall Flats. Playing out a favourite scene together, playing it and playing it.

But I had to know how the book turned out. Our futures were going to depend on it, one way or another.

And if he'd messed with that final scene…

I thought about that as I headed towards the library. And eventually it occurred to me that I was worrying over nothing. That he couldn't have played around with that scene or else it would have gone and Marge and I could not be living it. I had never lived in a first draft, and had no intention of starting now. The future might forever be uncertain, but the past was going to last until the pages that held me, held both of us, crumbled into dust.

The assistant was standing at the counter like he was waiting for me to walk in. He beamed a smile and I knew that at last the book was there.

I said, "It made it, then?"

"I read it last night."

"It's a good one, isn't it?"

"The critics are divided."

"What about the public?"

He raised his eyebrows. "Initial sales forecasts are impressive. It could be the big one of the series."

"So who cares what the reviewers say?"

"Not the public, obviously."

"What about you – did you like it?"

"He'll never top *The Black Widow*."

He led me to the hallowed place. The line of twenty one Miller mysteries, all lined up in chronological order. I went to the end of the row. I stood there, looking at it – *The Man Upstairs* – there on the shelf.

Waiting.

I took it down.

They'd kept the jacket design in line with the rest of the series, all pulpy and lurid. The library assistant asked if I needed anything else, but I think he already knew the answer to that. He left me alone and I sat myself down and went straight to page one.

Don't ask me how the miracle is performed. But there I am, reading a fiction constructed by another mind, knowing that none of it is true and that none of these people are real, and none of the places either – knowing full well that neither I nor the place that I'm sitting in reading it exist...and yet...I'm there, living it, breathing it, rising and falling with the punches...how can it be? How does it work?

I was deep into it when the assistant came back with some papers in his hand. He said, "I'm knocking off in a few minutes. I've copied some reviews - thought you might be interested."

I thanked him and wished him good night.

His grin was about as wide as Thomas Jackson's belly when he said, "Goodnight, Frank."

I sat back, the book finished and resting in my lap. TMU hadn't changed a thing. It read exactly as I remembered it, with not a line or an action out of place.

I picked up the reviews but they didn't keep me busy long. Some liked it and some didn't, and that was about all that there was to say. Of course, some made a meal out of saying it, but that's what they get paid to do.

At the bottom of the pile of reviews was something I *did* read.

An interview with TMU.

He spent half of it rapping on about how he'd not been well, and how the writing of this particular tale had been entirely therapeutic. How he thought at one point that he was going crazy; thought he shouldn't be writing books but seeking professional help.

Then he said how at some stage in the process of writing the book, he saw the light. The series had taken some turns that he hadn't thought out; turns that had been symptomatic of what had been going on inside him over a period of time. That far from going crazy with this book, it had been the end of a long tunnel. The "emergence from night into daylight" as he put it in that writerly way of his.

Most of the way through the book he'd wanted to scrap it; then at the death he'd realised that for the first time in his life he had got it absolutely right. He even called it his proudest achievement.

The interviewer moved onto the much publicised negotiations with the publishers. What had they insisted on changing?

TMU said that it came down to the scene with Miller and Jackson. The publishers hadn't liked any of that scene, preferring the idea of the mayor killing Frank.

TMU admitted that he had at one stage seriously considered going for that ending. The interviewer asked what changed his mind.

"Looking at my career in the long term, I kill off Frank – what do I do with the rest of my life?"

"Didn't the publishers see that? Didn't they want to protect their - and your - greatest asset?"

"You'd have thought so, wouldn't you? But I think they saw even greater profit in a new Chapeltown. They thought Frank was getting tired and clichéd and that another hero would pump new life into the series."

"They wanted the series to go on with Jackson as the main character?"

The interviewer reported that TMU became slightly emotional at this point, and merely nodded through distinctly misty eyes.

"You think the reading public would have accepted the victory of a character as immoral, as…*evil* as Thomas Jackson?"

TMU regained his composure. "Unfortunately, yes."

"But you didn't actually kill Thomas Jackson in the end, did you? Does that mean he will be back?"

TMU had then taken a pause for dramatic effect before answering the question. "I can exclusively reveal that Thomas Jackson, Elected Mayor of Chapeltown, died later from his injuries."

TMU had lost none of that wicked humour that had first brought him to the attention of the public. The interviewer started another question, but TMU came in on it.

"I find it a shame that people who have lived in Chapeltown from time to time, over the course of twenty novels, could embrace such revolution. I prefer to think that it could not have really happened that way. That had the publishers got their wishes, the public would have rejected the book. There would have been the initial feeding frenzy that comes these days with anything that has my name on the jacket, naturally. But I would like to believe that ultimately the book would have been rejected by the world and my name forever despised."

"So when they agreed to Frank Miller gaining the upper hand and defeating Jackson, what other changes were suggested?"

"Oh, well then it was going from black to white. They wanted a huge scene. A real in-your-face climax. I mean we're talking Hollywood now. The mayor getting the upper hand, Frank turning it around, the women - the Chapeltown Angels - getting butchered, buckets of blood and gore, armies of police, the Town Hall on fire, a car chase –"

"Involving a Datsun Cherry!"

"You don't like Japanese cars?"

"I –"

"You name it, they wanted it. Reams of the stuff. Another fifty pages minimum. And just when you think it's never going to end, bring on the false ending, Frank appearing to kill the mayor, then Jackson getting up again – so make that another dozen pages until everybody's sick of the whole damned thing. Can you imagine? They couldn't see that it was never that kind of a book. It's a strange book, no doubt about that. But sometimes that's okay. Sometimes you have to move out of your comfort zone and bring on the changes."

"Are you now fully recovered?"

"Recovered? From what?"

"Your recent illness."

"Never had a day's illness in my life. Don't believe what you read, son – and that's sound advice coming from a writer."

"But – you said –"

"And don't believe what you hear, either."

I could almost hear TMU chuckling between the lines. If he ever had been ill, it was sounding to me like he was on the mend. The interviewer went on. "Do you rate it as Frank Miller's finest hour?"

"Naturally."

"Is that because it's his latest – your latest – and you feel that you have a duty to promote it?"

"It's Frank's finest because it's his last."

"You mean his latest?"

"I mean his *last.* It's the end of the road for Frank Miller."

"This promises to be the biggest seller of them all - and yet you intend to finish the series?"

"I have finished the series."

"You won't be persuaded to reconsider?"

"Would you?"

"I…"

"Not in this life..."

Sometime later I was back at the flat with Marge. I wanted to engage in one more piece of nostalgia. It involved filling up a couple of glasses and getting her changed back into those fine white pyjamas.

I had some thinking to do and a lot of time to do it. TMU might be intending leaving me to replay this scene forever. And for the time being that was okay. A good deal more than okay in fact.

For now blue had turned to white. I loved the white but then I had loved the blue too, and was still in love with the memory. But all things must change. That much I did know. That much I had learned.

I'd heard rumours that eternity could last a long time, but in the case of Frank Miller it didn't have to be that way. TMU was a writer and he would never give up until the blood stopped beating through his veins. *The Man Upstairs* had given him back his life and that was some leverage for me when the time came. There was no hurry. Like me he needed a rest. The public too. But one fine day he would be back at his desk, pencils freshly sharpened, notepad pristine. And he would glance over his shoulder before making his new beginning; and I would keep my silence until the engine was running. And then he'd hear an old familiar voice.

Frank Miller could be relentless; it was the way he was made.

In the end TMU would give up fighting and come home for good.

He had signed off for now, consigning me to an imagined eternity in a world of white pyjamas that one day just might turn blue again.

But all things come to an end, in Chapeltown as in any town.

And so I took my leave.

But Frank Miller would be back.

Oh, yes: *Frank Miller would be back…*

THE END

44836475R00148

Printed in Poland
by Amazon Fulfillment
Poland Sp. z o.o., Wrocław